A lost treasure trove, (
determined to find the

Treasure hunter an
Bonebrake needs a vac.   ... things never seem
to work out as planned.

When a dying man gives him a treasure map, Bones finds himself on the run from the Knights of the Golden Circle, a secret society that will stop at nothing to find the treasure. But they are not alone in their quest for the lost riches. Also standing in his way are a historical revisionist bent on tearing down one of history's most beloved heroes regardless of the truth, and a true believer willing to preserve the legend at any cost.

Lost treasure, secret codes, and historical conspiracies. It's all in a day's work for Bones.

Praise for David Wood

"With the thoroughly enjoyable way Mr. Wood has mixed speculative history with our modern day pursuit of truth, he has created a story that thrills and makes one think beyond the boundaries of mere fiction and enter the world of 'why not'?" David Golemon, Author of the *Event Group* series

"Jurassic Park meets Jungle Cruise in this rollicking adventure!" Rick Chesler, author of *Golden One*

"*An* adrenaline-fueled thrill ride!" Alan Baxter, author of *Hidden City*

"What an adventure! A great read that provides lots of action, and thoughtful insight as well, into strange realms that are sometimes best left unexplored." Paul Kemprecos, author of *Cool Blue Tomb* and the *NUMA Files*

"David Wood has done it again. Within seconds of opening the book, I was hooked. Intrigue, suspense, monsters, and treasure hunters. What more could you want? David's knocked it out of the park with this one!" Nick Thacker- author of *The Enigma Strain*

"Dane and Bones.... Together they're unstoppable. Rip roaring action from start to finish. Wit and humor throughout. Just one question - how soon until the next one? Because I can't wait." Graham Brown, author of *Shadows of the Midnight Sun*

"A page-turning yarn blending high action, Biblical speculation, ancient secrets, and nasty creatures. Indiana Jones better watch his back!" Jeremy Robinson, author of *SecondWorld*

"A twisty tale of adventure and intrigue that never lets up and never lets go!" -Robert Masello, author of *The Einstein Prophecy*

"Let there be no confusion: David Wood is the next Clive Cussler. Once you start reading, you won't be able to stop until the last mystery plays out in the final line."- Edward G. Talbot, author of *2012: The Fifth World*

ALAMO GOLD

A Bones Bonebrake Adventure

DAVID WOOD

Alamo Gold by David Wood
© 2021

ISBN : 978-1-950920-28-0

Edited by Melissa Bowersock

Published by Adrenaline Press
www.adrenaline.press

Adrenaline is an imprint of Gryphonwood Press
www.gryphonwoodpress.com

Books and Series by David Wood

The Dane Maddock Adventures
Blue Descent
Dourado
Cibola
Quest
Icefall
Buccaneer
Atlantis
Ark
Xibalba
Loch
Solomon Key
Contest
Serpent
Eden Quest (forthcoming)

Dane and Bones Origins
Freedom
Hell Ship
Splashdown
Dead Ice
Liberty
Electra
Amber
Justice
Treasure of the Dead
Bloodstorm

Adventures from the Dane Maddock Universe
Berserk
Maug

The Elementals
Cavern
Devil's Face
Brainwash
Herald
The Tomb
Shasta
Legends
Destination-Rio
Destination-Luxor
Destination-Sofia

Jade Ihara Adventures (with Sean Ellis)
Oracle
Changeling
Exile

Bones Bonebrake Adventures
Primitive
The Book of Bones
Skin and Bones
Lost City
Alamo Gold

Jake Crowley Adventures (with Alan Baxter)
Sanctum
Blood Codex
Anubis Key
Revenant

Brock Stone Adventures
Arena of Souls
Track of the Beast

Myrmidon Files (with Sean Ellis)
Destiny
Mystic

Sam Aston Investigations (with Alan Baxter)
Primordial
Overlord
Crocalypse

Stand-Alone Novels
Into the Woods (with David S. Wood)
Callsign: Queen (with Jeremy Robinson)
Dark Rite (with Alan Baxter)

David Wood writing as Finn Gray
Aquaria Falling
Aquaria Burning
The Gate

David Wood writing as David Debord

The Absent Gods Trilogy
The Silver Serpent
Keeper of the Mists
The Gates of Iron

The Impostor Prince (with Ryan A. Span)
Neptune's Key
The Zombie-Driven Life
You Suck

From the Author

First, a quick heads-up: If you don't read to the end, you're likely to be left with a false impression about some of my views. If you're a reader who gets offended and stops reading because you think you've figured out the author's political or religious "bias", you're wrong.

Sometimes, when I'm traveling, I look around and think, "What kind of trouble cold Bones get into if he were on this trip?" This happened on a recent road trip I took with my wife, and the result is this book. It was a blast to write, and it gave me a chance to delve into history and conspiracy theories (which is kind of my thing.)

As always, I've changed a few details for the sake of the story and any actual places and people who appear in the story are fictional takes on the real thing.

Finally, thanks to Sean Sweeney for advance reading the early manuscript and to Melissa Bowersock for her assistance in cleaning up my messes!

Happy reading!

David

Prologue

William Travis stood in the San Fernando Bell Tower and gazed into the darkness as if he could look out over the miles and see the approaching army. The acrid smell of wood smoke burned his eyes, and the chill night air made him shiver. Never before had he been so keenly aware of his own mortality.

A massive army under the command of President General Antonio López de Santa Anna was marching toward the Alamo. Reports put their numbers anywhere between two and six thousand fighting men. Thousands of trained soldiers against fewer than two hundred Texians and Tejanos. Death was at their doorstep and steps had to be taken.

"I won't do it, and that is final!" The man in the coonskin cap stood, arms folded, glaring at Travis. Even in that ridiculous hat, Crockett projected an aura of strength and resolve. He was a difficult man at the best of times.

"There's no guarantee help will arrive in time. This must be done."

Defending the Alamo had not been the original plan. Sam Houston had ordered the fortress abandoned and its cannons moved to a more defensible position. But they lacked the draft animals necessary to move the artillery, and their orders had changed. Now they waited and prayed for help.

"You've got two hundred men to choose from. Ask one of them."

"You know what's waiting out there. Thousands of

enemy troops, not to mention marauders, Indians. Name one man other than yourself who stands a chance of getting through."

"Jim Bowie."

"Already asked him. He threw a knife at me."

Crockett chuckled. "If that's all it took to turn you in my direction, I can do the same. I warn you, I'm not as accurate as Bowie. Even if I tried to miss, I might end up cutting off something you would prefer to keep."

Down in the street, a beautiful young woman hurried past. She glanced in the direction of the tower, flashed a tiny smile. She lowered her head when she saw the men looking.

"There are other reasons for you to leave," Travis said.

"That is none of your business." Crockett watched her walk away, sadness shining at the corners of his eyes.

"You're not even a Texian. This is not your fight."

Crockett turned and glared at him. All traces of sadness were gone from his expression, replaced by a look that was something like pity. "I spent enough time in Congress to know there's more honor in the fight you choose than the fight your country chooses for you." He turned, rested his arms on the rail, and heaved a tired sigh. "I cannot abandon my comrades."

"Damn your pride, Crockett! You know what is at stake here. The future of Texas could depend on it."

"There is a difference between pride and honor, Travis. Maybe if you knew the difference, you'd command a bit more respect."

Travis bit back a scathing retort. It was true. He lacked the reputation and charisma of a Bowie or a Crockett. But he was the commander, and he would be obeyed.

"You're an intelligent man," Travis said. "What does Texas need more? A single rifle, or…"

"All right, I'll do it!" Crockett raised his hands in mock surrender. "But I have full say over how it's done."

"Agreed." They shook hands.

Crockett stared at him for a long time, his expression unreadable. Finally, with a sad sigh, he let his head hang.

"They will believe I abandoned them. All but the few who know their piece of the plan."

"I will make sure they know the truth," Travis said. "After the battle is won."

1

Bones Bonebrake crinkled his nose and waved away a cloud of acrid blue smoke as he made his way through the crowded bar. The walls were adorned with faded photos of actors from old Western flicks, and the décor was decidedly cowboy themed. The patrons were clad in urban cowboy gear, with lots of ten-gallon hats and oversized belt buckles on display. He was met with a variety of frowns, surprised glances, and even a few muttered curses. A six-and-a-half-foot tall Cherokee, broad of shoulder and powerfully built, was not a common sight.

He looked around and spotted the person he sought sitting in a corner booth nursing a mug of beer. At least, he looked like the man in the photos, a wizened Latino with leathery skin and long, silver-streaked black hair which he wore in a long braid. The old man glanced up, spotted Bones, and waved him over.

Bones had not taken two steps when someone barred his way. He looked down at the barrel-chested man who stood before him. The fellow was big, six feet tall, well over two hundred pounds, and not all of it was body fat. His t-shirt bore an image of a lion superimposed over a cross. It was only on second glance Bones realized the cross was formed from silhouettes of semiautomatic rifles. Weird.

"What the hell kind of Indian are you?" The sour stench of dipping tobacco was strong on his breath.

"The kind that has places to go and people to see and no time for bullshit."

The man blinked and took a step back. "I didn't mean no offense." He glanced around, saw people staring, and his cheeks went crimson. He took a deep breath, puffed out his chest, and bowed his arms. "But if there's a problem, I'll take care of it."

Bones strongly considered punching the man square in his unprotected face, but he did not need the hassle. And he detected a glint of fear in the man's eyes. Doubtless, he was accustomed to using his bulk to intimidate people, but Bones was a former Navy SEAL and did not scare easily.

"There's no problem, bro." He forced a smile and winked. "You enjoy your night."

Satisfied, the man stepped aside as Bones shouldered past him. "That's what I thought."

"By the way, your old lady said to tell you she'll be home late. I'll take good care of her," Bones called over his shoulder.

It took a moment for his words to sink in. The man let out a stream of curses and made to come after Bones, but two of his friends grabbed him by the arms.

"Let it go, Shane," one of them said. "Remember you're already on probation."

Combined, the two men probably did not weigh as much as Shane, but he pretended to struggle to break free of their grasp.

"Settle down, Shane," the second man said. "Besides, you ain't even got no old lady. She moved in with your brother last year, remember?"

This managed to redirect Shane's ire in his brother's direction. Still spewing epithets and vowing revenge against his sibling, he allowed himself to be frogmarched over to the bar.

Shaking his head, Bones turned to see that the old man whom he had arranged to meet was no longer seated at his table. Looking out over the crowd, he caught a glimpse of silvery braided hair. The man was making a beeline for the back of the pool hall.

"That doesn't make sense. Dude literally told me to meet him here." And then spotted another man moving toward the rear of the establishment. He was blond, clean-shaven, and his flannel shirt and boots looked like they had been bought off the rack at the local big box store that very day. He looked even more out of place here than Bones did.

Alarm bells ringing in his mind, Bones followed him. It took a while for him to navigate the throng of drunks. A buxom woman of early middle years offered to buy him a drink. When he politely declined, she flashed a disappointed smile then pinched his ass as he walked away.

"I guess this place isn't all bad," he said, smiling to himself.

The men's room stank of smoke, urine, and ammonia. Discarded paper towels overflowed the garbage can in the corner and spilled out onto the floor. The lone toilet stall was open, the door dangling by a single hinge. There was no one in sight. His eyes moved to the open window. There was no way Bones could squeeze through it, but the old man might have managed it without too much difficulty. Bones stuck his head through and looked up and down the alleyway. There was no one in sight.

"Mister Gonzales?" he called.

He heard a loud thump against the wall to his right. Muffled voices filtered through the cheap paneling.

"Give me the map," a man's voice said.

"I don't know what you're talking about." He recognized Gonzales' voice from their conversation on the phone the previous day.

"I know you have it. Your brother told me."

"My brother is dead."

"I know that. You're welcome."

Gonzalez let out a cry and Bones heard the sounds of a struggle. He dashed out of the bathroom. Beside it was a door marked STORAGE. Upon it hung a sign that read DON'T MESS WITH TEXAS. He tried the knob and found it locked. He could still hear voices and the sounds of a struggle. The old man was in trouble. He took a step back and threw his weight into it. Sharp pain burst through his shoulder. Damn! This door might be the only solid structure in the entire pool hall.

He looked around for help, maybe a staff member with a key, but he was around a corner out of sight. Someone behind the door let out a cry of pain. Bones knew he was out of time. He slammed into it again and felt the door facing shatter.

Inside, Gonzales lay amongst boxes of paper towels and toilet tissue, his hands pressed to his stomach. Blood oozed between his fingers. There was a security door in the back that stood slightly ajar. Bones ran to it and looked outside. He heard the faint sound of running feet, but the alley was empty.

He returned to Gonzalez and examined the man's injury. It was a deep belly wound, the kind that hurt like seven hells before it killed you.

"You're going to be all right," he lied, tearing a strip off the old man's shirt, folding it up, and pressing it to the wound.

"No time for lies," Gonzales panted. "Take the map."

"What map? I thought we were going to talk about alien abductions." Bones loved conspiracy theories of all kinds. He and Gonzalez had bumped into one another online and the old man had invited Bones to meet for a couple of beers should he ever find himself in Houston.

"In my boot." The old man grabbed Bones by the collar. "Don't let them get it."

"Let who get it? Was it the blond man?"

Gonzales tried to speak, but he could not manage the words. His eyes fluttered, then closed. His body sagged limply against the wall. Bones pressed his fingers to the man's wrist but felt no pulse.

"Holy freaking crap." Here was Bones, a stranger in town, kneeling over the body of a dead man, a man whom Bones had arranged to meet. If he were discovered, he would probably find himself locked up for a very long time awaiting a trial. He was not about to wait around for that if he could help it. He was innocent, and the murderer was getting away.

He pushed the door closed, then hurried back to Gonzales. He pulled off the man's left boot and checked inside. Nothing. He checked the right. It was empty, too. Or was it?

Through the insole, he felt an indentation. He lifted it to find a hollowed-out space in the heel of the boot. Inside was a folded sheet of paper. Before he could examine it, he heard someone at the door. Bones ducked behind a stack of boxes and waited. The handle turned and Bones held his breath. A large figure appeared in the doorway. It was Shane, the wannabe bully with the weird shirt. Shane staggered inside, closed the door behind him, and began fumbling around for a light switch.

"There's no light in the head!" Shane called out to no one in particular. The man was too drunk to realize he had missed the men's room by one door.

Bones smiled. Here was his chance to get a little revenge on this assclown and make a clean getaway. *Killing two rednecks with one stone*, as his uncle Crazy Charlie used to say.

He crept up behind the unassuming drunk and delivered a right cross that turned his lights out. He hastily dragged Shane's limp body over to where the dead man lay. Let the idiot explain what he was doing lying beside a dead man. He slipped the old man's boots back onto his feet. Then, being sure not to leave fingerprints, he crept out the back door and closed it behind him. He ran down the alley, cursing his luck.

"Can't even have a beer with a fellow conspiracy theorist without running into trouble."

2

Bones hurried through the alley, eyes peeled for the man who had killed Gonzales. He moved on silent feet, a skill he had learned from his grandfather growing up in Cherokee, North Carolina, and had later refined in the service. He saw nothing, heard nothing but strains of country music from the pool hall and the blare of a distant horn.

He rounded the corner onto the side street where he had left his Ram pickup in the parking lot of an abandoned strip mall. Inside, he unfolded the paper he had recovered from the old man's boot and gave it a quick glance.

"What in the hell is this?" There were a few lines and shapes that might be a map to something, but there was no context for them. They could have been anywhere in the world. He had only a moment to take it in before a small sedan, a Toyota hybrid of some sort, flashed past him, flying down the street. The driver was blond with a gaunt face. Bones recognized him immediately.

"That's the guy."

He fired up the engine and followed at a distance. The sedan was far ahead of him. Bones floored it and the pickup truck slowly gained ground on its quarry.

The driver took turns seemingly at random, cutting through the dark streets. They were in a mixed business and residential area that showed signs of urban decay. Most of the buildings were dark, with FOR SALE signs out front. Here and there he saw lights on inside a dilapidated house.

Bones wondered how long he could follow without being noticed. Probably not much longer. He and his quarry were the only vehicles on the road right now. He eased off the gas and tried to keep the car in sight.

Finally, the hybrid came to a stop in front of a rundown Gothic style house. It was completely dark inside. The cracked windows and unkempt landscape told him the building had not been occupied in some time. Bones parked on the side of the road a short distance away and cut the lights and engine. He watched as the driver got out, looked around, then hurried inside.

"This is not your problem," Bones said to himself. As usual, his curiosity and sense of justice got the better of him. He took out his phone and snapped photos of the hybrid and the building. Next, he looked up the address. The search results revealed that the house had most recently been a real estate agency belonging to a man named Stetson Rice but had closed years ago. No help there. If he was going to learn anything, he would have to do it himself.

Nothing moved on the first floor. He spotted a flickering light in a second-floor window. It looked like someone had lit a candle. At the corner of the house, a trellis ran up to the second floor. He tested it and found it sturdy enough to support his weight. He was an experienced climber and scurried up spiderlike. He peeked inside the window where he had seen the light.

The blond man's back was to Bones. He knelt before a makeshift shrine—votive candles and a framed black-and-white portrait of a man. Bones did not immediately recognize him, but the image rang a bell. The room contained a folding cot and chair. A suitcase stood in the corner beside a cooler. There was nothing here to give him a clue as to who this man was, or what he wanted with the map. He was debating his next move when a voice called from the street.

"What are you doing up there?"

He looked down to see a bearded man in tattered clothing pushing a shopping cart. One of the many homeless people who camped beneath the city's network of elevated highways. He tried to wave the man away, but the man was having none of it.

"You ain't supposed to be up there."

Inside, the blond man snapped his head around. Their eyes met.

"Holy crap," Bones said.

Two things happened at once. The blond man drew a pistol, and the trellis gave way beneath Bones' feet. He barely had time to let out a curse before his feet struck the ground hard. He rolled and came up running. A shot rang out and a bullet pinged the cracked pavement at his feet. He veered to his left, taking him out of the line of fire, then rounded the parked car and made a beeline for his truck.

The homeless man stood with his shopping car in the middle of the street. Bones had only a moment to wonder what the hell he was up to before he reached beneath the bags in his cart and took out a sawed-off shotgun.

Bones had only a split second to make his decision. Instinct told him he could not get away in time. Instead, he charged.

The man racked a round and lowered his weapon just as Bones collided with the shopping cart, knocking the man off his feet. He flew backward, his shotgun booming as it flew through the air.

Another shot rang out, this time from the house, and a bullet whizzed overhead. Bones kept running, weaving to make himself a more difficult target to hit. A third shot and a bullet tore through a SLOW CHILDREN AT PLAY sign. If Bones' friend Dane Maddock had been here, Bones would have wondered aloud where all the slow children were. But he had no audience at the moment. A shame. He reached his truck, fired it up, and put it in reverse. His tires squealed on the pavement as the Ram shot backward along the darkened street.

The blond man dashed out of the house and ran for his car. Bones' Glock was tucked beneath the front seat. He drew it and fired left-handed through the open driver's side window of the moving vehicle. The shot went high, shattering one of the bay windows of the old house. The blond man hit the deck, buying time for Bones to whip the truck around and tear off down the empty street.

Seconds later, he saw headlights behind him. The man was giving chase. Bones put the pedal to the floor. The pickup lurched forward.

He drove blindly through the decrepit neighborhood, taking turns at random, keeping an eye on the headlights of the pursuing vehicle. It soon became apparent that he could not outdistance the hybrid. Instead, he shut off his headlights and barreled down a one-way street. It then became a game of cat and mouse as Bones took turn after turn, trying to lose his pursuit, but to no avail.

Finally, he spotted the interstate in the distance, a series of raised roads high above ground level. He had no idea where the on-ramps were.

"This city has too damn many bridges," he muttered.

Headlights closed in behind him. The man was catching up. A shot rang out and a bullet smashed through the only working streetlight.

"If I can't get away from this asshat, I'm going to have to find a place to make a last stand," Bones said.

Up ahead, a village of tents had been set up on a berm that lay between the road and a shallow drainage ditch that ran beneath the highway.

"Bingo."

The Ram bounded over the curb with a loud thump and a bump. Urban campers scattered as the pickup rumbled through their tent city.

"Sorry!" Bones shouted at the angry people who cursed him and made obscene gestures.

In the rearview mirror, he saw the hybrid scrape over the curb in a shower of sparks, ripping the air dam off the front bumper. The Toyota skidded and fishtailed in the soft earth. Bones shifted into four-wheel drive and took his truck into the canal, emerging on the other side where an access road led to the on-ramp of the interstate.

Behind him, the Toyota went full Dukes of Hazzard, flying through the air but failing miserably to make it over the small concrete river. Bones laughed with relief as he headed up onto the highway.

"I wonder what an ordinary life is like?"

3

Stetson Rice limped through the tent city, headed back toward the old house where he currently made his home. All around him, homeless people stirred like ants in an upset hill. They shouted curses at him as he walked past.

"Damn hobos," he muttered. "It's not like I killed one of them. I didn't even knock over their tents." He kept walking, eyes straight ahead. Why did society waste precious resources on the likes of these, who only took but gave nothing back? Couldn't anyone see the bigger picture?

"What you gonna do about your car? You just can't leave it there!" A man with red hair and brown teeth thrust a crooked finger in the direction of the crashed vehicle, which was now stuck in the canal.

"It's not mine," he said without looking back. That much was true. He'd rented it with a fake ID and credit card, and he was careful to always wear gloves when he drove it. Hell, he was wearing them right now. When the cops found the totaled hybrid, the rental papers would point to a Sam Pond from Pennsylvania. Pond was a real person. Rice and Pond had once gotten into an argument online about green energy tax credits. Pond would not concede the argument, so Rice had stolen his identity.

He hurried away from the camp, walking as fast as pride would permit. There were a hell of a lot of vagrants down here, perhaps more than he could deal with in a fight. He was halfway down the block when he heard footsteps behind him. He turned to see two of the hobos stalking toward him. One carried a knife, the other a club.

"What's your problem?" Rice asked. If push came to shove, he carried a snub-nosed .380 concealed and had two rounds left. That would be all he needed.

The man with the club, balding with skin and eyes the same shade of mahogany, grinned. "I'm Curtis."

"Are we going to be friends, Curtis?" There was no warmth in Rice's tone.

"That all depends on you," Curtis said. "You see, we got a good look at your face. We figure we'll follow you to wherever you're going. That information ought to be worth something to somebody, don't you think?"

"The insurance company doesn't care which way I walked," Rice said. "Now why don't you two fellows piss off?"

"Ain't no call for that," said the knife-wielder. "No reason we can't make a deal."

Rice blinked. The speaker, whom he had taken for a small man, was in fact a bald chick. And she appeared to be the more dangerous of the two. Her eyes were clear and glinted with mischief.

"A deal?"

"Our silence is for sale. And we come cheap." Her laugh was gentle and feminine, her eyes big and blue. Rice could tell that she had once been a great beauty before life had taken its toll. "We saw you chasing that man and we heard the gunshots. We got his license plate, too. Me and Curtis, we're the smartest of the bunch."

"Of that, I have no doubt," Rice said dryly.

"Anyhow," Curtis began, scratching his chin, "the police is bound to come around sooner or later."

"Are you on Groupon? I'm low on cash at the moment."

The pair exchanged glances, then laughed.

"You're funny," the woman said. "My name is Susie, by the way."

"Nice to meet you. I'm Jose Altuve."

The two laughed when they heard the name of the Houston Astros second baseman.

"If you're a ballplayer you could do with a bat." Curtis held up his club, a sturdy length of pipe. There was a relaxed air about him, but he kept a tight grip on the makeshift weapon.

"Fine," Rice said, a plan forming in his mind. "Look, that guy I was chasing, he assaulted my sister a few years back and got away with it. When I saw him tonight, I lost it and chased after him. He shot at me, but I was so pissed off I couldn't think straight. I just wish he would come back. What I wouldn't give to be able to bash him in the head with that bar."

"I suppose we could include it in the deal," Curtis said, laughing. "For the right price."

"So, what is the going rate for hobo discretion?"

Susie frowned. "We don't like that word. Hobos live on trains. We're just regular people who are down on our luck."

"Sorry," Rice said. He didn't give a damn what they liked. He just needed to keep them at their ease for just a bit longer. "Name your price."

"A hundred bucks, and it's locked in the vault forever." Susie ran two fingers over her lips in a zipping motion. "Two hundred and we'll make sure everybody in the camp tells whatever story you like."

"Another hundred and I'll let you have my bat, Mister Altuve," Curtis added. The man surely had at least one more weapon hidden on his person.

Rice nodded. To someone with a bit more faith in humanity it might have sounded like a sweet deal, but Rice knew that humans were primarily motivated by self-interest. Loyalty lasted as long as it was convenient and profitable. Even if he bought them off, this wouldn't be the last he saw of these two. Doubtless, they planned on shadowing him home so they could also use that information to extort him.

"I wish I could afford the full meal deal, but I'm a little short on funds." He took out his money clip and began counting out bills, watching the two homeless out of the corner of his eye, ready to draw his pistol at a moment's notice. He peeled off five twenties, a ten, and six ones.

"How much will one sixteen get me?"

"We'll tell the cops the driver of the car was a Mexican with his hair dyed blonde," Sue said. "And we'll point them in the wrong direction."

Rice didn't miss the glance Curtis flicked in Susie's direction. They thought he was an idiot.

He held the wad of bills out toward Curtis, who made the mistake of letting go of his pipe with one hand when he reached out for the cash. Rice dropped the bills, jabbed his index and middle fingers into Curtis' eyes, then snatched the pipe away before the money touched the ground. He dodged Susie's awkward knife thrust and caved in her skull with the pipe. The shaved-headed hobo skank hit the ground like a fainting goat. Rice wasted no time. He flung the pipe at Curtis, who ducked. He used the distraction to grab Susie's knife and plunge it into Curtis' heart.

It took the man a moment to realize he was dying. Disbelief shone in his eyes, his lips moved, and he slowly sank to the ground. Rice quickly placed the knife and bat in positions that would suggest the two had killed one another. He hastily collected his cash, then strode off down the street with a hop in his step. Two more roaches crushed under his heel.

4

Bones checked into a public campground a short distance off the interstate. It was after hours, which meant he did not need to interact with staff or anyone else for that matter. Payment was made by leaving cash in an envelope and placing it in a drop box. He chose a remote campsite, far from the other campers, and settled in for the night.

The moon shone through thin clouds, sprinkling the pine trees with silver light. Sweat rolled down his back and the humid air made everything feel damp and sticky.

"Tonight's weather, muggy with a chance of mosquitos," he muttered.

He didn't bother with his tent. Instead, he doused himself with mosquito repellent and bedded down in the back of his truck. At least there was an occasional breeze out here. Maddock would have strung a hammock between two pines and slept there, but hammocks were for old people and guys with man buns.

He took out the map and examined it under the beam of his flashlight. The first thing he noticed was that the paper, though creased and worn, was not all that old. And the various lines and markings appeared to have been written at different times. Some were in pencil, the rest in black or blue ink. A row of hand-drawn images ran along the bottom of the page. They were barely more than doodles, really. No artist had sketched these. But what were they? If they had been scattered among the forked series of lines that covered the page, he would have taken them for landmarks. But drawn where they were, he was uncertain of their significance.

Perhaps if he copied them, he could gain some insight. He took out a small notebook and, one by one, sketched out the images: a bird perched on a stone, a woman with praying hands, a figure atop a pedestal, a blocky shape with a hump in the middle, and a few more. When he had finished, he looked them over again, even turning it upside down for no particular reason. Nothing helped.

Next, he examined the lines that covered the middle of the page. As with the images, there was no context to help him identify what this was a map of. It resembled a system of rivers, with feeder branches coming in and out. But was that it and if so, where was it?

Realizing he wasn't going to make any progress like this, he snapped a photograph of the map and texted it to his friend, Jimmy Letson. Jimmy was a reporter for *The Washington Post* and an accomplished hacker. He had a knack for digging into databases undetected and had assisted Bones and his friends on similar treasure hunts. He typed out a quick message.

Yo, Jimmy. I dare you to match this up to an existing map. Bones

The reply was immediate.

I'm not that easily manipulated. Just for that, I'm doubling my fee. Two bottles, and not the cheap stuff. Jimmy loved Scotch whisky.

It all tastes like corpse water, Bones texted back. He was more of a beer and bourbon man. He added a vomit emoji. Jimmy was a nerd and nerds liked that sort of thing.

Jimmy's next reply gave him little hope. *Do you seriously expect me to match these few squiggly lines to anything at all? And they're hand-drawn, which means they're likely to be imprecise.*

Are you saying you can't do it, or you won't do it? Bones fired back.

Screw you, Uriah.

Bones gritted his teeth. He hated his given name. He shook his head. Jimmy was probably right. The odds of matching this document to any known map were slim. Furthermore, Jimmy only had access to things that had been digitized and stored in a database. But maybe he could help in a different way.

He asked Jimmy to look up Alberto Gonzalez, the deceased UFO hunter who had given him the map. And then he remembered something he had heard in the pool hall earlier that night. The man who had killed Gonzales claimed to have killed Gonzales' brother, too. Maybe he, and not the UFO enthusiast, had created the map. He asked Jimmy to follow up on that as well, and as an afterthought he attached a photo of the old house and the vehicle the killer had driven, then added the address.

See what you can find out about this.

You don't want much, do you? You're going to owe me a case by the time I get done.

Bones chuckled and texted back. *Only if you succeed.*

Jimmy replied with a poop emoji.

"Nerd," Bones said with a grin. Satisfied he had done all he could for the moment, he stretched out on his foam mattress, closed his eyes, and descended into fitful slumber.

Bones awoke to the sound of an approaching vehicle. He sat bolt upright, his hand going to his Glock. Footsteps approached. Whoever this person was, they were trying and failing to move with stealth. Bones vaulted out of the bed of his truck, putting the vehicle between himself and the new arrival. He melted into the shadow of a pine tree and waited.

It was a solidly built man wearing a police uniform. Holy crap! Had Bones already been linked to the killing of Gonzales? Or might this be about the chase through town? He watched as the officer circled the pickup truck, shining his light inside, testing each door to see if it was unlocked, then inspected the license plate and gave a nod.

Bones decided it was time to face the music. "Is there a problem, officer?" he said, stepping out from his hiding place.

The man jumped a foot in the air, stumbled, and dropped his flashlight. He steadied himself against the truck for a moment. "It's Constable," the man corrected, picking up his flashlight, which appeared to be broken.

"My bad," Bones said.

"What were you doing hiding in the woods?"

"Just coming back from the latrine." Bones pointed with his thumb in the direction of the pit toilets that stood off in the distance behind him. When the wind was just right, he could smell it from here.

"I didn't hear you coming," the constable said, clearly annoyed.

"I'm an Indian." Bones left it at that.

The constable peered down into the bed of the truck, shone his light across Bones' mattress pad. He frowned. "When people come to campgrounds, it's usually for camping."

"I've got a tent, but I decided I'd rather deal with the mosquitos than with the stifling heat." Bones was having doubts about this alleged officer of the law. His uniform was ill-fitted, with only a few generic-looking patches. He carried a revolver in a leather holster and wore blue jeans and cowboy boots. None of it looked like standard issue to Bones, but who could say what passed for normal in some parts of the country? Still, it didn't feel right.

"I'll need to inspect your vehicle," the constable said quickly. "Can you unlock it for me?"

"It's not a crime to sleep in the bed of your truck."

"But theft is?" The man flashed a smug grin.

"Theft?"

The constable nodded. "There was an altercation tonight at a pool hall in Houston. You know anything about it?"

"I don't know much about much," Bones said. "I'm just passing through."

The constable frowned, a sly look on his face. "Where you headed?"

"Amarillo," Bones invented on the fly.

"Coming from Florida?" the man asked, glancing at Bones' license plate. "Took a strange route, didn't you?"

"I hit Galveston for a couple of days. And no offense, but your beaches don't compare to Key West."

At the mention of Galveston, the constable flinched. He suddenly grew excited. "I'll need to see inside the vehicle immediately. And you'll have to be searched, too."

"No problem. Just as soon as you show me some credentials."

"This is the only credential I need." He tapped his badge and took a step forward. Funny how the most aggressively confident people were usually the charlatans and liars.

It was the reaction Bones had expected. This guy was a fraud. Once he had the map, he would have no reason to leave Bones alive. This needed to be dealt with immediately. Bones feigned compliance, made a show of leaning forward and squinting to get a better look at the badge. As he did so, he inched closer.

"Sorry, I'm just trying to read the fine print."

And then Bones attacked. His big hand closed around the smaller man's wrist, seizing control of his gun hand. With his right hand, he grabbed the man by the collar and head-butted him in the face. He felt the man's nose break, heard his squeal of pain, smelled the coppery scent of blood as it began to flow. The man tried to break free, but Bones was too strong and too skilled a fighter. He drove his knee into his opponent's crotch, eliciting a squelch like stepping on a jellyfish. As the man sank to his knees, Bones disarmed him.

It was a Ruger Redhawk with rosewood grips. A beautiful weapon, but not one Bones would have chosen for serious action. It was a double-action, but Bones thumbed back the hammer for effect and took aim at the man's face, finger on the trigger. Just a twitch and a .44 caliber slug would dig a trench in the fake cop's skull.

"You wouldn't dare," the man said.

"When they find you, you'll just be another cop who drove out to an isolated location and ate his service revolver. It happens all the time in your line of work." Not that this asshat cared about the demons that often plagued those who put themselves on the front line. He was a fake, a criminal, a wannabe killer.

"I'm not a cop." The man's eyes went wide at the inadvertent admission.

"No shit, Sherlock. I want you to listen very carefully. I know ways to hurt you that you can't imagine in your darkest nightmares, and I hate assassins. So, you had better answer my questions. I can tell when someone is lying or holding something back. Learned it from a shaman." That part wasn't true, but scared white people tended to believe that sort of crap about Native Americans, and Bones took full advantage. The man swallowed hard and nodded. "Who are you, really?"

"Don't kill me. My name is Houston Austin, and I'm not an assassin. I manage a sporting goods store. I'm on the deacon board of Lion Gate Church."

Bones winced. "Seriously? What's your middle name? Staubach?"

Austin shook his head. "It's Ryan. After Nolan, the ballplayer."

"All right Mister Austin, why are you poking around my truck?"

"You know we want the map," Austin said.

"Who is we?"

Austin's face went pale, and he trembled. "I can't tell you. They'll kill me."

Bones fired at the soft earth between the kneeling man's legs. It kicked up a spray of dirt and elicited a yelp from the kneeling man.

"You could have shot me in my…" He couldn't bring himself to say the words.

"You see, that's the difference between me and them. I won't just kill you." Bones' voice was as cold as a senator in a winter power grid failure. He bared his teeth in a predatory grin. "Last chance."

Austin looked around in desperation, probably hoping that campers had heard the gunshot and that help was on the way. But this was rural Texas, where the occasional gunshot didn't quite draw attention the way it might in a big city or a suburb back East. As he twisted around, the top button of his shirt popped open, revealing a medallion on a leather cord. Bones snatched it and held it up. It was a bronze medallion, old and worn smooth by time. An eight-pointed star stood at the center with lines radiating out behind it forming a Maltese Cross. He could just make out what had once been words, numbers, and a design around the edge.

"I take it this is the symbol of your order?" He could tell by the way Austin averted his eyes that he had hit the mark. "What is it called?"

"The Knights of the Golden Circle." Austin's voice trembled as he said the name.

"Are you an important man in this group?"

Austin shook his head. "I'm low man on the totem pole. Sorry," he added with a nervous glance at Bones.

"My tribe doesn't do totem poles, but thanks just the same. That was surprisingly courteous for someone who was planning to kill me."

"I just want the map. I swear."

"Have you seen the map before?"

Austin shook his head. "I was told to retrieve a map you stole off a dead man. But they didn't tell me what it looked like. I figured I would grab anything that looked old."

"The map leads to something old, then? What is it?"

Austin looked him in the eye. He was white as an Icelandic girl in the dead of winter, and he trembled like a hipster waiting for the craft brewery to open. He took a deep breath and whispered a single word.

"Treasure!"

5

Bones rolled down the window and drew in a deep breath of the salty Gulf air. It was early evening in Galveston, and traffic was light in the old town district. A popular tourist destination, Galveston, Texas had once been a major international city and one of the busiest ports in the United States. It had been dubbed the Wall Street of the South and had competed with New Orleans as the most important port city on the Gulf of Mexico. That had all changed at the dawn of the Twentieth Century, when the island was devastated by the Galveston Hurricane of 1900. The natural disaster was still considered the deadliest in United States history, with an estimated death toll of six thousand to twelve thousand people. The island's fortunes waned but eventually rose again when, with the advent of Prohibition, Galveston reemerged as a center of tourism and illegal gambling.

As he drove along, Bones admired the architecture of the many old buildings that comprised the East End Historic District. These days, people were far too quick to tear down an old building instead of investing in preservation.

He still didn't know the name of the man who had murdered Gonzales. Jimmy's investigation had revealed that the man appeared to be operating under an assumed identity. He confirmed one thing Bones had already learned—the building in which the man appeared to be living belonged to an elderly Houston area real estate magnate. No help on Alberto Gonzales or his map.

Austin had also proved to be a poor source of information. He was a low-level operative who knew little about the organization of which he was a member. The meetings were conducted in remote locations and all the participants wore hoods to protect their identities while they debated strategies for preserving their version of the "American way of life." Sort of like a KKK Comic-Con. The group took its name from a secret society founded in 1854 whose objective was to create a nation called the Golden Circle; one in which slavery would be legal. The golden circle would have been comprised of the Southern United States, Mexico and Central America, South America's Gulf Coast, and the islands of the Caribbean. The order had faded from existence after the Civil War.

The man knew precious little about the treasure he and his society sought. All he knew was this it was a cache of gold, silver, and jewels worth millions. What was more, the treasure held tremendous symbolic value, though he couldn't say why. Members of his order used the shorthand Texas Treasure when discussing it.

One of the few bits of helpful information Austin had given him was that, according to members of his order, Galveston and the map were linked somehow. That dovetailed nicely with the one helpful bit of information Jimmy had turned up—Alberto Gonzales' brother Jorge had been found dead in Galveston, the victim of an apparent suicide. Operating on those clues, Bones had traveled to Galveston in hopes of matching the images on the map. After catching a few hours of sleep, he had hit a couple of bars, buying drinks for old dudes and listening to their stories, occasionally dropping in a discreet question in hopes of finding a match. He had finally come up with one possible connection—one of the drawings bore a striking resemblance to a tomb in the Old City Cemetery.

He arrived at the cemetery shortly before the last ghost tour of the evening was about to begin. He decided to join the tour. Tour guides could be useful sources of information. As he approached the group of tourists, he spotted the guide and stopped short.

"No freaking way!"

Kendra Gill was a tall, lithe woman with a creamy complexion, big brown eyes, and wavy chestnut hair. She was a paranormal investigator whom Bones had met when he and Maddock had searched for King Solomon's Mines. Their eyes met and she did a double-take, then laughed.

"Bones Bonebrake! I can't believe it," she said, hurrying over to hug him. "It's good to see you. How's Maddock?"

"He's boring, as always. Hanging out with his social media influencer girlfriend instead of hunting for treasure like a real man."

"Oh." Kendra's eyes fell for a moment. Bones had forgotten that she had a thing for his friend.

She brightened almost immediately. "But if I remember correctly, you are much more open-minded about ghosts than he is."

"That's true. The only thing I'm closed-minded about is the French. They suck."

Kendra laughed through her pained grimace. "Never change, Bones."

"Does that include my boxers, because this humidity is giving me swamp crotch."

"I did not need to know that. I think I'll begin the

tour now. Want to join?"

"When the guide is as cute as you? Absolutely."

The tour was entertaining and informative. The Old City Cemetery was two centuries old, making it the oldest burial ground in the region. Filled with mausoleums and ornate nineteenth-century tombs, the graveyard was a memorial to Galveston's varied and often bizarre history.

"The Broadway Cemetery District consists of seven cemeteries," Kendra explained. "There are three layers of burial plots, holding over twelve thousand sets of human remains."

"They were buried on top of each other?" a boy in a Deadpool t-shirt asked.

"Space is limited on the island, and most people prefer burial to cremation. So, they did the best they could with what they had."

As she guided them through the graveyard, Kendra pointed out the older and more ornate gravestones, those with interesting epitaphs, and those that were associated with hauntings.

There was the grave of Elize Roemer Alberti, who murdered her four children in 1894, earning her the moniker "the demented mother." According to legend, she was possessed by a demon, leading her to poison her children and eventually take her own life. The modern take was that she suffered from post-partum depression and trauma from other losses in her family.

"Alberti was buried with her children," Kendra said. "At night, visitors have reported hearing her children's anguished screams, and her sobs of regret."

The stories kept coming. Cutthroat pirates, notorious brothel madams, a Confederate deserter buried upside down in an unmarked grave. Even a cannibal had found his final resting place on Galveston Island.

As the tour was ending Bones finally spotted what he had been looking for. It was a large vault, arched in the center. It reminded Bones of a stylized replica of the famed Alamo mission.

He hung back while Kendra bade goodbye to the tour participants and accepted their thanks and gratuities. When she was finished, she made her way over to where he waited.

"I hoped you would hang around. Want to grab a drink and catch up?"

"I'd like that. But there's something I need to do first. As long as you don't snitch." He gave her a wink.

She frowned. "What are you up to, Bonebrake?"

"It's probably better if you don't know. Maybe you could keep a lookout for me?"

"Not until you tell me what's going on." She folded her arms and tapped her foot, waiting.

Bones looked around to make sure no one was nearby, but now that the tour had ended, he and Kendra were the only people in the cemetery. "I'm on a treasure hunt, and I think that tomb over there might be a clue."

Kendra's eyes went wide. "That one? You can't be serious."

"What's the problem?"

"That is the grave of Ezra Cornwell, one of the survivors of the Battle of the Alamo."

"I thought everybody died at the Alamo."

She shook her head. "All of the defenders fought to the death, or were captured and executed, depending on which account you believe. But lots of people survived the battle: women, children, slaves, a few older men. Cornwell was part of the latter group."

"Maddock would find that interesting, but what's up with your reaction? You look like you just saw an alien, or Nancy Pelosi naked."

Kendra let out a tiny laugh. It was cute. "Politics aside, I'll take the alien. But to answer your question, there's a whole lot about this tomb you ought to know."

6

"**The tomb of** Ezra Cornwell is famously haunted," Kendra explained as they made their way over to it. "People have reported feeling someone grab them, or hearing someone whispering in their ear, but they can't understand what's being said."

"Have you investigated it? I know that's your jam."

"I've tried to connect with his spirit a few times, even made some recordings trying to capture EVP."

Bones nodded. EVP was an acronym for Electronic Voice Phenomena, recordings of what paranormal investigators claimed were spirit voices.

"Any luck?"

She shook her head. "All I got were the words 'fire rocket' over and over."

"Maybe you picked up a signal from NASA? They're not far from here."

"That would be something, wouldn't it? I do believe there's something supernatural at play here. I'm highly attuned to such things and I always get a chill when I visit this grave."

They reached Cornwell's tomb and Bones took out his flashlight and shone it upon the weathered white marble. He scrutinized every inch of the exterior while Kendra continued to fill him in the history of the gravesite.

"There are more ornate and interesting graves, in my opinion, but this is the one people ask about most often. They examine it just as closely as you are doing right now. Some of them just sit down in front of at and stare in wonder, like they've just completed a pilgrimage or something. Sooner or later, they all give up and leave."

"Any idea why it's so popular?" Bones asked.

"The long-timers say it's the Alamo connection. It's one of the most significant moments in Texas history."

Bones nodded, but he was only half listening. There was something he had just noticed about the layout of the graveyard.

"There are eight obelisks surrounding this tomb," he said, shining his flashlight around in a circle.

"That's significant?"

"Look at how precisely spaced they are. That can't be by accident. And if you were to plot them on a map..." He knelt and poked eight holes in a patch of soft earth. "Then connected them like this..."

Kendra understood immediately. "It would form an octagram, or an eight-pointed star. In Egyptian mythology the eight points symbolized the four male and four female deities. Each pairing symbolized one of the primal forces: air, water, darkness and infinity. All together they represent the sun god Ra. In Wicca it's one of the ways to represent the Wheel of the Year."

"Wheel of the Year? Is that the book series Maddock read for two decades and wound up hating the ending?"

"Not exactly," Kendra said. "What does the symbol mean to you?

"To the Native American in me, it represents hope and knowledge. The sailor part of me sees a compass rose."

"I can tell you there's no treasure hidden in or beneath the tomb. Some real estate bigwig financed a thorough investigation. Excavation, ground penetrating radar, the remains were examined. Nothing."

Bones considered this new bit of information. If a real estate tycoon had financed the investigation, that was a potential link to the man who had murdered Gonzales. It also suggested that he was in the right place.

"I think this tomb is part of a map that points the way to a treasure."

"Who made the map?"

"I think it was a group called the Knights of the Golden Circle." He reached inside his shirt and took out the medal he had taken from Austin. "Have you seen this symbol before?"

She bit her lip, her brow furrowed in thought. Finally, she shook her head. Bones' heart sank. And then Kendra's expression brightened. "Yes, I have! And not long ago." She cast a furtive glance around.

Bones was immediately on alert. "What is it?" he said, looking around.

"Nothing. It's just the memory of what happened creeped me out." She took a deep breath. "A lot more people than usual have been checking out this particular grave recently. I joked that we ought to wall it off and charge a fee to see it. Not everyone thought it was a bad idea. Anyway, I was about to leave for the night when two guys started fighting right in front of the tomb. One guy pulled out a gun and then the other fellow did this." She twisted her left hand and contorted her fingers in a claw shape. "And the other dude stopped right there. Lowered his gun."

"Then what happened?" Bones asked. His heart was racing.

"The dude with the gun said, 'Oh Lord, my God.' But he said it like a question."

"Let me guess. The other man replied, 'Is there no

help for the widow's son?'"

"Yes!" Kendra nodded enthusiastically. "And then they both turned and looked in my direction. I was hiding but it was like they knew someone was there. They came in my direction, and I hid in the only place I could."

"Where was that?"

"The dumpster. I watched them while they searched all around. One of them passed close by my hiding place and I saw a medallion like that one, but newer and cheap looking, like they ordered it off of Wish. Finally, they gave up and agreed they hadn't actually seen or heard anyone. They climbed up onto the tomb, looked around for a while, then left." She shivered at the memory. "I'm not trying to be a drama queen, but I swear they would have killed me if they found me."

"You might be right," Bones said. "The Freemasons have a secret symbol, the Grand Hailing Sign of Distress. It's revealed only to those who achieve the rank of Master Mason. The exchange you heard was another way one Freemason would ask another for help."

"Oh, come on. Freemasons are guys like my uncle. He joined because he owns a small business and it's a good way to make connections. I can't see him killing somebody for revealing a hand sign."

"You're right," Bones said. "For the average Freemason, the secret signs and symbols are little more than a test to determine who is trustworthy and who has a big mouth. But I know more about them than the average person, stuff I'm not supposed to know, and what you showed me is not the distress symbol I'm familiar with. Are you sure about what you saw?"

"Absolutely. It was burned into my mind so

completely that I couldn't stop practicing it. Now I couldn't forget it if I wanted to." She rubbed her hands together as if she could scrub away the memory.

"Show me again."

Kendra repeated the gesture a few times and Bones copied it until he had it down pat.

"If it's not the Freemason symbol, what is it?" she asked.

"Many of the original Knights of the Golden Circle were also Freemasons. Could be they preserved some Masonic practices but added some of their own. I think you saw the secret distress symbol of the Knights of the Golden Circle."

7

Stetson Rice III found Austin's Ford Ranger pickup abandoned in the forest near a campground west of town. All the tires had been slashed, including the spare. The ignition wires had been ripped out, the taillights smashed, and the license plate was missing. There was a strong odor of gasoline in the air. He looked under the vehicle and saw that the fuel lines had been disconnected and the tank drained. He had to admire the thoroughness and efficiency with which the task had been accomplished. The whole job probably hadn't taken more than two minutes, but it guaranteed Austin would be going nowhere any time soon.

The obvious question now was what had become of Austin. If he was dead, there would be no reason to disable his vehicle. This was his last known location. He had to be here somewhere.

Rice searched the ground in an ever-widening circle, looking for footprints. After ten minutes he gave it up. Whoever parked the truck had moved like a ghost, leaving no trace of his movement. Perhaps he'd swung from the trees like Shia LaBeouf in that last Indiana Jones movie.

"It has to be the Indian," he muttered.

Rice had used connections within the organization to learn that the man he had chased the previous evening was named Uriah Bonebrake. He was a former Navy SEAL who now lived in Key West and ran a treasure-hunting outfit along with some other vets. The revelation that Bonebrake was a treasure hunter had sealed the deal for Rice. He didn't know if the man had gotten onto the trail of the Texas Treasure, but Rice was determined to stop him.

"Where the hell are you, Austin?" Austin was not a valuable man by any stretch, but he was a loose end that needed to be tied up one way or the other.

A gentle evening breeze stirred the sultry evening air, carrying with it a stench like death. Rice tensed. Had he just caught a whiff of Austin's remains? In this weather, decomposition began quickly.

He followed the fetid breeze until he came to a row of outhouses. "Pit toilets," the campground called them. He crinkled his nose and spat on the ground.

"I'm never going to find that imbecile." He was about to leave when he heard someone speak.

"Help?" The voice was hoarse, faint, so soft he wondered if he had imagined it.

"Austin?" he said tentatively.

"For God's sake, help me!"

"Where are you?" He waited. No answer. "Austin, tell me where you are."

He waited through another five interminable seconds of silence before he finally got a reply.

"I'm in the shitter."

"You don't need my help with that."

Another long pause, and then a forlorn groan. "Dammit, Rice, just come see for yourself."

The pit toilet was comprised of a wooden shack with three doors. For some unknown reason, they had been designated for MEN, WOMEN, and FAMILY. Rice rolled his eyes. They were just holes in the ground with seats placed over them. Why did they need to be gendered?

The men's and family stalls were empty. In the women's room, Rice found a disgusting sight. Austin had been stripped to his skivvies, hogtied, and dumped in the pit toilet. Lucky for him, the toilet was in an out of the way location and saw little use. Still, the young man was coated in filth. The sight and smell made Rice retch.

"How did this happen?" he grunted.

"That damn Indian got the drop on me. Took everything and dumped me in here." He hesitated. "He even stole my grandfather's medallion."

Rice shrugged. "It's not like it's a secret that the Knights existed. He stole a family heirloom, which was a crappy thing to do." He paused. "Sorry, I don't mean to make light of your situation."

Austin didn't quite meet his eye. He was hiding something.

"What did you say to him?"

Austin hesitated, swallowed hard. "Nothing important."

Rice stood up straight, icy calm washing over him. He drew his .380 and aimed it down into the pit.

"Please, Rice! He didn't give me much choice. I held back as much as I could."

"Tell me everything you said to him," Rice said coldly. "If I'm satisfied you aren't lying to me, then maybe we'll discuss getting out of there."

Ten minutes later, he emerged from the toilet, absently trying to brush the stench off of his clothing. He took out his burner phone and dialed a number he knew by heart.

"Austin squealed," he said without preamble. "He didn't tell him much, but he pointed the Indian toward Galveston. Keep an eye on Cornwell's tomb. That's the one spot we know for certain is on the map. If he's on the hunt, he's bound to show up there sooner or later."

"You want him eliminated?"

"Only if you can do it discreetly, and only if you have the map in your possession."

"What about you?" the voice on the end of the line asked.

"I'm going to be delayed. I've got a mess I need to clean up here."

8

Bones examined the oddly shaped tomb where the Knight of the Golden Circle had been laid to rest. It had obviously been constructed to resemble the Alamo in a general way, but there were some obvious differences. It was square, whereas the Alamo mission was more rectangular in shape. Also, each corner was surmounted by a stone ball.

"You said the guys you saw climbed up onto the tomb?"

Kendra nodded. "Crawled all over it, inspected every inch. From the disappointed looks on their faces, I got the impression they didn't find anything."

"I think I'll take a look," Bones said. "Keep an eye out for me."

Traffic flowed past them, residents and tourists going about their business. No one, however, seemed to be paying any attention to what was happening in the old cemetery. That was okay with him.

Bones climbed up onto the vault and took a quick look around to make sure no one was watching. He took out his flashlight and switched it to the red beam, better for sneaking around at night. The red light was not visible from a distance the way an intense white beam would be.

As he had feared, there was nothing on top of the vault. He got down on his hands and knees and checked for fine lines that might have been washed away by time, ran his fingers across the surface, but he felt nothing. He moved to the nearest corner and gave the ornate globe a similar inspection. This time, he felt something. Just a few lines that might have once been an engraving. He took out a notepad and pencil and made a rubbing. Faint lines appeared on the page. He held them up to the light and could just make out the word LEGION and an arrow. He grinned. Legion was one of the words that appeared on the great seal of the Knights of the Golden Circle.

Buoyed by this discovery, he made a rubbing of each globe. Two of them were so eroded that he got nothing more than a few straight lines. On the opposite corner, he could discern the word UNION and another arrow. Pleased, he hopped down and shared his discovery with Kendra.

"I don't mean to be a downer, but we already knew that Cornwell was a Knight. This just reinforces that."

"The arrows aren't part of the seal, and they both point in the same direction. I thought maybe we could follow in that direction and see where it takes us."

They crossed the cemetery in the direction the arrows pointed, but nothing they encountered seem to relate to the mystery. Finally, they decided to pursue a different avenue of investigation. Bones showed Kendra the map to see if any of the symbols drawn at the bottom were familiar to her. One, a raven sitting on a gravestone, caught her eye.

"I know exactly where this one is." She led him a short distance away to a gravestone that matched the sketch. Any date or epitaph that had been engraved on the tomb was long gone, washed away by the years.

"Do you know anything about this one? Any legends or ghosts associated with it?" Bones asked.

Kendra shook her head. They looked it over, made

rubbings of some of the smooth surfaces, but found nothing. Disappointed, Bones stood and looked around.

"I don't suppose there are any other raven tombs around here are there?"

"Maybe in another cemetery, but definitely not this one."

Bones cast a baleful glance at the carved bird as if it had offended him. This had to be the correct grave. The raven was perched in the exact spot as shown in the drawing, his head was turned at the same angle, gazing off into the distance. Bones circled in front of the bird folded his arms and stared into its eyes.

"What are you looking at, ugly?" he said to the bird.

"Maybe that's it!" Kendra said.

"What do you mean?"

"It looks to me like the bird is staring in the same general direction as those arrows pointed."

Bones nodded, stroked his chin thoughtfully. "So, if we can identify all the symbols on this map, maybe together they point to a single location."

"That's what I'm thinking. Maybe we should…" She halted midsentence, frowning.

Bones saw immediately what had caught her attention. Four men were lurking around his pickup truck. Telltale bulges beneath their clothing told him that all were armed.

"I recognize one of those men. He was the one who flashed the secret sign. Do you think they're the Knights of the Golden Circle?"

"Got to be," Bones said. "I think we should get out of here before we're spotted. Where are you parked?"

Kendra laughed. "I ride a bicycle. Not an automobile kinda girl if I can help it. Saves money, better for the environment."

"That's just great." He took her by the hand and led her across the cemetery, headed away from the Knights lurking around his vehicle.

"Don't be rude. I'm trying to save the Earth," she said.

"Yeah? Well, I'm trying to save your ass." He glanced back. Two of the men had broken away from the group and were following them. Another pair remained beside his vehicle.

Kendra looked up at him and smiled sweetly. "Playing the hero. Isn't that sort of what you do?"

"Not intentionally, but it always seems to work out that way." Bones considered his options. He didn't like his odds in a gunfight. And when secret societies were involved, who could say how far their reach extended? Throughout history, groups like the Illuminati managed to infiltrate every segment of society. Their reach extended into law enforcement, the justice system, the Armed Forces, and the government. The notorious Catholic archdiocese of Boston sex abuse scandal had been covered up for many years by Catholics in various branches of government who valued the institution above the individual victims. Perhaps the same was true for the Knights of the Golden Circle. It was a risk he did not want to take.

They began to run through the cemetery, keeping behind the cover of the tombs and crypts in case somebody decided to start shooting. Bones looked back and saw that the men were giving chase. Even if he and Kendra could outrun them, neither of them was faster than a bullet. Something had to give.

"We need a way out of here, and I'm seriously

considering carjacking somebody."

"Don't do that," she said. "I have another idea."

9

They left the cemetery, rounded a corner, and found themselves staring at a big yellow boat on wheels. It was covered by a bright blue canopy. A handful of tourists waited inside for the ride to begin. It was a bizarre sight. A sign read *Duck Boat Tours.*

"Follow my lead," Kendra said. She climbed aboard and slid into the driver's seat.

"We're hijacking this thing?" Bones said. "Awesome! But shouldn't I drive?"

"No, I need you to grab that mic and serve as the tour guide," Kendra said.

"But I've never been to this town before."

"And I've never driven a big yellow amphibious vehicle while being chased by armed members of a secret society, so it's a big day for both of us." She shifted the boat into gear and hit the gas. With a sputter and a rumble, they pulled away from the curb.

Bones looked in the direction of the office, but the staff members were busy helping customers. He wondered how long it would take them to realize a tour had left without them.

"Took you long enough," a man in the back row grumbled.

"Sorry about that," Bones quipped. "It takes a lot of work to look this good." He pretended to smooth his hair. The women on board laughed and a few eyed him lasciviously. He relaxed a little. He was good with an audience. He could do this.

In the distance, the two men who had been following

them were just leaving the cemetery. They were way behind. Perhaps he and Kendra could get out of this without any serious trouble. In order for that to happen, they had to sell this as a normal tour. No drawing unwanted attention. He picked up the mic and improvised.

"Good evening ladies, gentlemen, and financial burdens." The parents on the tour chuckled. "Welcome to the rolling boat tour. First of all, I'd like to assure you that this vehicle is, in fact, seaworthy. On that note, we do offer rides to any politicians who want to escape Texas before the weather turns cold and the power grid fails." This comment elicited a few laughs. A few others sat in silence, their faces twisted in deep thought as they tried to decide whether it was okay to laugh at self-serving politicians regardless of party affiliation, or if they were obligated to defend any action taken by someone from "their" side. Bones knew how this story would end. One of them would eventually come up with a "What about…" for the "other side" and that would soothe their troubled minds for a while. He hurried on.

"But let's talk about happier things, like the amazing tour you're about to take." Kendra turned the boat onto the main coastal road. The street sign read *Seawall Boulevard.*

"This is Seawall Boulevard. It was named for the famous graffiti artist Angus Seawall, who never saw a wall he didn't want to paint. Or maybe it's just because there's a big seawall over on that side of the road. Experts disagree." More laughter.

"You're good at this," Kendra said as she hit the gas and the vehicle lurched into traffic.

"Thanks. Thinking on your feet is important in my

line of work."

Bones racked his brain for anything he knew about Galveston. The research he had conducted paid off, as he discussed the city's founding, heyday, and the tragedy of the great hurricane. He pointed out the obvious landmarks, reading their names off the signs outside, and inventing bits of trivia.

"You are a wonderful guide," said an elderly woman seated near the front. "I have been on this tour several times and never heard any of these interesting facts."

"It's just one of the many services I offer," Bones said in a mildly flirtatious tone. He was relaxing now that they appeared to have eluded the Knights of the Golden Circle. "Does anyone have any questions?" he asked the group.

"Why is the water here brown?" a young man asked, pointing out at the moonlit gulf.

"Supposedly it's silt from the Mississippi River being carried along by the current, but we all know it's because too many Dallas Cowboys fans vacation here." He said this with a wink and a nod to a man in a Houston Texans cap. Someone else asked about a giant shark statue they had seen in another part of town. Wanting to atone for his earlier political joke, he explained that it was a replica of the shark that ate Joe Biden's memory. This seemed to soothe any residual butthurt among the passengers. He was actually having a good time.

And then the sound of a gunshot shattered the calm.

Screams rang out. Along the street, people scattered, seeking shelter behind parked cars or inside the many businesses that lined the island's coast.

Bones looked back and cursed. In the distance, the men who followed them were flying down the road on scooters, weaving in and out of the vehicles that cruised Seawall Boulevard. He ducked as one of them took hasty aim and fired again. The bullet went wide, shattering the rear window of a white SUV parked along the side of the road.

In the back row of the boat, the man who had earlier complained about the delay in leaving sprang to his feet. He wore a pistol at his hip, which had escaped Bones' notice up to this point. The man whirled about and drew his pistol. The safety must not have been engaged because, in his haste, he fired a shot down through the floor. Passengers screamed and tried to move away from him.

"Get down, Kyle!" a woman lying on the floor shouted.

Unnerved, Kyle tried to take aim, but his hands were too shaky to control his weapon. Another shot rang out and he hit the deck.

"I can't do it," he said.

Bones breathed a sigh of relief. In a crisis situation, an armed and untrained civilian typically posed as much of a threat to the people they were trying to protect as did an armed criminal.

"Can you get us out of here?" he said to Kendra.

"Traffic sucks, but I'll try." With that, she veered the rolling boat into oncoming traffic. Horns blared, tires skidded, angry voices cried out as the big yellow boat careened down Seawall Boulevard. Bones was thrown to the deck. He got to his knees and peered over the dashboard to see a travel bus coming right at them. Its horn let out a deep, throaty blare as it closed in on them.

"Holy crap!" he shouted.

Kendra yanked the wheel hard to the left, missing

the bus by inches and taking the boat up over the curb and onto the wide sidewalk.

They rumbled past the tour bus, then swerved back over to the right side of the road. All the while, their pursuers continued to fire on them as they closed the gap on the strange boat.

"Is the shooting ever going to stop?" Kendra shouted. "It's like they don't care who they hit."

"They don't care. Let the idiots keep firing. They'll find it difficult to change magazines while driving a scooter." Bones' words proved to be prophetic. A couple more gunshots, then both weapons went silent.

"Thank God," Kyle, the man with the pistol said. "I thought I was going to have to take care of business."

"If you draw that weapon again, I'll take it away from you and spank you with it," Bones said. He was in no mood for wannabe heroes. The Knights might have run out of ammunition, but they were still coming. The scooters zipped along the center line, their small engines emitting high-pitched whines. Vehicles made way as the knights closed in.

Decorating the tour boat were a pair of long wooden oars fastened to the port and starboard gunwales. They were there strictly for show but would do in a pinch. Bones ripped one free and rushed to the stern.

The Knights were almost upon them. The man in the lead must have saved at least one bullet because he raised a pistol and took aim. Bones thrust with the oar, taking the man in the chest just as he pulled the trigger. Like the loser at the joust, the modern-day knight was unhorsed. His scooter shot out from underneath him. In desperation he grabbed onto the oar, yanking it from Bones' grasp. It wasn't enough to save him. The Knight hit the pavement and rolled. His partner barely avoided crashing as he navigated around his fallen companion.

"It's called a lance! Hello!" Bones shouted.

"Is this part of the show?" said the young man who had earlier asked about the muddy Gulf waters.

"Yes, but it's almost over," Bones said. Sirens blared in the distance. The police were on their way. He hoped the Knights would break off their attack before they were caught.

No such luck.

There was a loud thump and gloved hands appeared clutching the port side gunwale. In a flash, a man leaped nimbly over the side. Impressive!

"What are you, a Romanian gymnast?" Bones said.

The man, athletically built, and dark of hair and eyes, grinned wolfishly and adopted a fighting stance. There was no room to circle, feint, or utilize any of a variety of fighting techniques. This would be a brawl inside a phone booth. Bones raised his fists and moved in.

His opponent was big, strong, and lighting fast. He slipped Bones' first jab and countered with a right to the jaw. Bones replied with a right cross that just missed then followed with a left to the rib cage the man absorbed with only a slight grunt of pain. The snapped two quick jabs that caught Bones on the cheek. They weren't powerful blows, just enough to sting, but man, the dude was fast!

Bones feinted a leg kick, nearly impossible to execute in such a confined space, but the man reacted to it, lowering his hands enough for Bones to land a hard left that wobbled the Knight in his tracks. Bones reached up, grabbed the bar that supported the boat's canopy. He swung forward, raised his knees to his chest, and kicked the man full in the stomach with both feet. The Knight flew backward and landed hard on the deck, but he recovered immediately. As he climbed up onto his hands and knees, he spotted Kyle hunkered down a few feet away, his pistol on his hip. The idiot hadn't engaged the safety strap on his holster. The Knight snatched the weapon free.

Bones had been reluctant to use his Glock in such a crowded place. Now he was regretting that decision. Nothing he could do about it now. Bones charged, knowing he wouldn't get there before the Knight squeezed the trigger.

Tires squealed and the world spun as Kendra made a sudden, hard left turn. The sharp report of the knight's pistol boomed in Bones' ear, but the shot went wide as the Knight fell against the gunwale. The man tried to regain his feet, but Kyle slammed into him. Both went tumbling to the deck. The Knight lost his grip on his stolen weapon, and it skidded across the deck.

"Nice one!" Bones said.

The boat car lurched over the curb with a loud thump and shot out onto a wooden pier. Tourists scattered, some vaulting over the side rails and plunging into the warm waters of the gulf as the boat fishtailed along the pier. Kendra was pumping the brakes and struggling to control the skidding vehicle.

The Knight shoved Kyle away and regained his feet, but this time Bones was faster. He drove his fist into the man's chin, stunning him. Bones scooped him up and flung him over the gunwale in a single motion. The man flew through the air with a strangled cry and hit the water amidst a chorus of cheers from the relieved passengers.

Kendra brought the boat to a stop just short of the end of the pier. The passengers began to applaud and whistle.

The old lady who had praised his tour guide skills earlier hugged Bones, gave him a peck on the cheek, and pressed a five-dollar bill into his palm.

"I don't know why these people are after you, but it's obvious you're one of the good ones."

"Why do you say that?"

"Those others, they didn't care who they hurt, did they?"

"That's right," said Kyle. "You two get out of here. We'll cover for you."

"Seriously?" Bones said.

"You saved our asses," Kyle explained, collecting his pistol off the deck and holstering it. Once again, he didn't engage the safety or secure it in the holster. Bones winced internally but let it slide. Kyle deserved a break after doing his part to stop the Knight.

"I'll tell them I took the boat for a joyride," said the old lady. "For years I've been trying to summon the courage to do it. That's why I take the tour so often." She plopped down into the driver's seat and smiled. "You kids hurry on out of here."

Bones thanked her, then turned to shake hands with Kyle. He reached out, but Kyle's eyes suddenly went wide. He drew his weapon and fired at Bones' head. There was no time to react. Bones heard the bullet zip past his ear like a supersonic hornet, heard a grunt and something heavy thump to the ground. He turned to see the Knight of the Golden Circle lying on the pier, a bullet through his forehead. A knife lay nearby.

"He was about to get you," Kyle said.

"Good work," Bones said. "I hope you don't get into trouble for it."

"Just standing my ground. Got lots of witnesses."

They shook hands and he and Kendra slipped away into the night.

10

Kendra lived in an efficiency apartment on the top floor of an old house in Galveston's historical district. Tapestries hung from the angled walls, and at the peak dangled crystals and glass globes. All around were candles, beads, and figurines representing cultures from around the world. The strong smell of essential oils hung heavy in the air. In one corner stood Kendra's ghost hunting equipment—an infrared camera, a high-tech digital voice recorder, and a few other items. Bones had seen some of it in action before, when Kendra had helped him and Maddock on their search for King Solomon's Mines. A second bookshelf was filled with a mix of new age, spiritual, and paranormal books. An antique kerosene lamp sat on a floating mantel above it.

They sat at a small folding table in the center of the room, dining on Mexican food they had ordered in, and enjoying ice-cold bottles of Dos Equis, Bones' favorite beer.

The television was on in the corner. Already the airwaves were abuzz with news of the wild chase and shootout along Galveston's major tourist strip. The media had taken and run with the story of the eccentric old lady who stole the boat and the hero citizen who stood his ground against domestic terrorists whose motives were unclear. Interspersed with the report were clips from traffic cams. Fortunately, the awning that covered the duck boat made it impossible to identify the driver or passengers. It seemed that Bones and Kendra were off the hook, at least for the moment.

"How am I going to get my truck back without eliminating the other two Knights?" Bones grumbled.

"No need." Kendra waved away his concern, her eyes locked on the television screen. "I texted my boss and told him I saw a guy selling weed in the parking lot just as I was leaving. He's got security watching over things now and the police are going to keep an eye on the cemetery."

Bones nodded, satisfied. He took a swallow of Dos Equis. Now it was time to figure out their next move.

Kendra had several tabs open on her laptop, each for a different tourism or historical site related to Galveston. So far, they had identified potential matches for the map symbols. Some were gravestones, others were statues or distinctive landmarks.

"I don't mind telling you the last few have me stumped," Kendra said, tapping her chin thoughtfully with the tip of her stylus. "If these are gravestones, they could be anywhere. Or they might represent locations that are no longer there."

"Maybe we don't need them," Bones said. An idea was forming in his mind.

"What do you mean?"

"Take a look at what we already have." He grabbed a souvenir map of Galveston and began marking the points they had identified, making a dot for each. When he had finished, the points he had plotted formed two parallel lines, each running from north to south across Galveston Island. He pointed to the spot where their search had begun.

"We know the arrow on Cornwell's tomb points this way." He drew in an arrow. "And the crow faces this way." He added another arrow. "Using the satellite images, we also know the directions a few of these statues are facing."

"I didn't think of that," she admitted.

"Just a hunch," he said, drawing in more arrows. "What do you see?"

"This one appears to be looking right at the Cornwell tomb," she said, indicating a spot diagonal from the tomb. "Except over a great distance."

"Exactly." Bones drew a straight line between the two dots. "And we've got a couple more pairs looking at one another." He drew two more lines. "And I suspect that if we were to find all of these places and visit them in person, every one of them would have some kind of arrow pointing to a spot on the opposite line of landmarks." He joined up a couple more dots. The lines intersected at a single point.

"So far, all of them meet in this spot in the middle of town," she said.

"Anything there?" Bones asked.

"There's a statue. I think it's worth checking out." She closed her laptop, stood, and began clearing the table. In doing so, she inadvertently knocked over Bones' beer.

Bones sprang to his feet with a loud curse as the frothy liquid spilled out over the table. He snatched the original map just before it was ruined but he lost his grip on it and it landed atop the scented candle Kendra had placed on the table.

"Dammit!" He grabbed the map and held it up away from the flame and the spreading liquid.

"I'm so sorry," Kendra said. "Is it all right?"

"Yeah, it's fine, it's…" He paused. His jaw dropped. "Holy freaking crap."

"What is it?" Kendra hurried to his side.

Symbols had appeared in the center of the map where it had lain over the candle. Just as quickly as they had come, they began to fade away.

"Oh my God! What are those?"

"Some sort of invisible ink," Bones marveled. "The ink must have been activated by the heat of the candle. I wonder what else we can find."

After clearing and drying the table, they lined up candles to generate as much heat as they could without endangering the document. Carefully, Bones held the map out over the candles and lowered it toward the heat until the lines appeared again. He moved the document from right to left, revealing more symbols that crossed the page.

"They are everywhere," Kendra whispered. "But they disappear so fast!"

"Grab your phone and get some pics," Bones said. "We'll take it a section at a time."

They took a systematic approach, as if working a grid on a dive. They started in the top left corner and worked their way across, heating every square inch of the page, exposing every hidden symbol. Kendra snapped photographs of each section until they had a visual record of all the secret markings. Next, they transcribed them onto a notepad as the original images once again faded away.

When they finished, they had copied three separate lines of code. There were some vague similarities between the three but none of the symbols were exact matches for any of the others.

"Secret societies and now a secret code!" Kendra said. "Hanging out with you is a lot of fun. Except, of course, when people are trying to kill me."

"It's part of the all-inclusive Bones experience," he said. "I'm even better after dark."

"Because it's harder to see your ugly mug?" she said.

"Ouch."

She reached up and patted his cheek. "Just teasing. You're actually quite cute." She gave him a chaste kiss on the cheek then returned her attention to the lines of code. "Do you think these are three different codes or just one long code?"

He counted the rows of symbols. There were twenty-six of each. He grinned. "I think we've got three separate codes here, simple substitution for the letters of the alphabet. If we can break any one of them, we can break all three."

"So, it's like a Rosetta Stone for secret societies," Kendra said. The Rosetta Stone was an ancient Egyptian stele dating back to nearly two hundred years before Christ. It contained an official decree written in hieroglyphics, demotic script, and in ancient Greek. It had proved essential for scholars to finally decipher Egyptian texts.

"Exactly right," Bones said.

"So, how do we figure it out?" she asked doubtfully.

"Some of the symbols ring a bell. I'll bet I can decipher it. But first I want to take a look at that statue."

11

The Texas Heroes Monument was located at the intersection of Broadway and Rosenberg Avenue in the heart of Galveston. Commissioned in the late 1800s by financier and philanthropist Henry Rosenberg, it commemorated the brave souls who fought in the Texas Revolution. It was originally unveiled on April 22, 1900. The monument stood seventy-four feet tall. Its bulk consisted of a square marble pedestal adorned with a bas-relief sculpture on each face, topped by four columns fifty feet high. At the top of each column were inscribed words which represented the qualities of those who fought for Texas: Courage, Honor, Devotion, and Patriotism. The statue was surmounted by the twenty-two foot tall figure of *Lady Victory*. She stood facing north. In her left hand, she clutched a sheathed sword wrapped in roses, symbolizing the beginning of an era of peace. She held a crown of laurels in her outstretched right hand, representing victory. Rising above the city, illuminated by the faint glow of streetlights, it was an impressive sight.

Bones and Kendra had recovered his truck from the cemetery parking lot. As they had hoped, the remaining Knights were nowhere to be seen. They parked in the drugstore lot at one corner of the intersection. Traffic was sparse this late at night, but they kept an eye out for prying eyes.

"I don't get it," Kendra said. "This is such a well-known monument, if there were treasure hidden here, wouldn't it have been found by now?"

"Not unless clues pointed the searcher in this direction. Even if you believed there was treasure hidden somewhere on the island, it could literally be anywhere. Every tomb, grave, statue, old building is a possible hiding place. Hell, any landmark or hole in the ground is a possibility. I've found some surprising things in unexpected places."

"That's what she said," Kendra said automatically.

"I like you," Bones said, grinning.

They circled the monument, inspecting each section. On the north side, at the base of the "Patriotism" column, was a bronze relief of Sam Houston flanked by representations of war and peace. Beneath were carvings of five Texas heroes of the revolution. Below them, affixed to the pedestal, was a bas-relief representation of the battle of San Jacinto.

The column devoted to "Courage" faced east. It featured a statue of a woman unsheathing a sword and ordering the Mexican army out of Texas. She was called *Defiance.* Below her was inscribed *October 2, 1835*, the date of the notorious Goliad Massacre, in which hundreds of Texan prisoners of war were executed by their Mexican captors, and a sculpture of the tragedy beneath it.

Facing west was the column called "Honor." The statue here was a bronze female figure who symbolized *Peace.* Names of heroes were listed at her feet and below her, a carving depicting Santa Ana surrendering to Sam Houston.

"I'm not feeling hopeful," Kendra said as they moved to the last side. "Nothing here stands out."

"We'll see," Bones said.

The south-facing side was titled "Devotion." It

featured a medallion of Stephen F. Austin flanked by allegorical figures representing heroes of the Alamo. Here, the bas-relief artwork depicted the last defense of the Alamo, showing the moment that Mexican troops broke through into the mission. An injured Jim Bowie lay on a bed in the corner, defending women and children.

"Where is Davy Crockett?" Bones asked.

"He's not there?" Kendra asked, moving closer. "Maybe he was fighting in a different part of the compound."

"Just seems weird," he said. "Crockett's a big deal and he's usually prominent in artistic representations of the Battle of the Alamo. Those I've seen, anyway."

He paused, stepped back, and looked the monument up and down. His gut told him that there was something here waiting to be discovered. The Cornwell tomb was designed to symbolize the Alamo, and the arrows atop had pointed in this direction. There had to be a connection, but what was it?

"What were the words you heard when you did EVP at the Cornwell tomb?"

"Fire rocket," she said. "At least, that's what it sounded like to me.

"Fire rocket," Bones repeated. "What if it was 'find Crockett'?"

"You think a ghost is whispering a clue to a treasure vault?"

"Probably not," Bones admitted. "But my gut is telling me that Crockett ought to be here."

"But he is." Kendra pointed up at the cherubim flanking Stephen Austin. "The one on the right is considered an allegorical representation of Davy

Crockett."

"Interesting." Bones narrowed his eyes and gazed up at the cherubim. The Crockett cherubim and his counterpart were staring off toward the west. Bones turned his head in that direction. There was a carwash there, but nothing else visible through the trees that surrounded it.

"Did you know you tug your braid when you think hard?" Kendra said.

"It's usually a ponytail," he replied automatically. "I'm going to climb up there."

"What if somebody drives by?" Kendra asked, looking around nervously.

"I know what it's like to live in a beach town. A dude climbing on a statue wouldn't be the strangest thing someone has seen in the middle of the night around here. Just warn me if anything seems weird."

"Seems weird," Kendra echoed. "Gotcha."

"You're sort of a smartass, you know that?" Bones said as he clambered up the white marble and swung himself up onto the base façade, then up onto the top of the pedestal.

"Kind of a pot and kettle situation, don't you think?" Kendra replied.

"See? That's what I'm talking about." Bones worked his way around the columns until he reached the cherubim that represented Davy Crockett. If he could just get up to eye level with it, he could see exactly where it was looking. He put one foot up onto the ledge where it stood.

"Five-oh!" Kendra exclaimed. She pointed south in the direction of the beach.

They turned to see a patrol car slowly coming in

their direction. He hastily circled around to the opposite side of the monument and hunkered down on the shelter of *Lady Peace,* while Kendra hit the deck, flattening out behind the scant cover of the landscaping that surrounded the monument.

The officer driving the patrol car must have had bigger fish to fry, or maybe he simply had no reason to look for people climbing a local monument in the middle of the night. Either way he cruised past them and was soon out of sight.

"Thanks for the warning," he said to Kendra.

"No problem," she said climbing to her feet and brushing leaves from her legs. "Ugh. I got pine needles in my mouth." She spat. "Not my worst Saturday night."

Bones chuckled as he balanced on the narrow ledge beside the Crockett cherubim. He put himself at eye level with the statue and pressed his cheek against it.

"That looks really creepy and inappropriate," Kendra said.

"You are supposed to be keeping a lookout." He narrowed his eyes and stared through the darkness, trying to see through the tall pines. Something was there.

"You told me to keep an eye out for anything weird and what you are doing right now definitely falls into that category."

"You always have a clever retort, don't you?" If he squinted, he could just make out the building, a large ornate one if his eyes did not deceive him.

"You can't possibly be this lacking in self-awareness," Kendra retorted.

"On the contrary, I'm very clear about my personality traits. I just don't like them in other people. What is the building over there?" He pointed in the direction the cherubim stared.

"That's the Moody Mansion. Belonged to some rich family back in Galveston's heyday. It's now a museum."

"Was it there when the monument was installed?" he asked.

"I'm not sure. Maybe."

Bones felt disappointed. His gut told him he was missing something. He took out his flashlight and shone the red beam up and down the cherubim looking for anything he might've missed. It felt weird giving such a thorough inspection to a statue of a boy in a loincloth. He was glad his friend Willis wasn't there to see it. There would be no end to the ribbing.

A flash of white light temporarily blinded him.

"That's a Kodak moment!" Kendra proclaimed, holding up her smartphone.

"I didn't know people still use that phrase," Bones said.

"I'm an old soul."

He took a moment to blink away the spots in his eyes and was about to climb back down when something caught his attention. The Crockett cherubim held a scroll in its left hand. Bones shone his light inside the scroll. If he angled it just right, he could see…

"Holy freaking crap!" What another person might have taken to be nothing more than part of the texture of the statue, Bones recognized as symbols from one of the codes on the map. They were so tiny and etched so shallowly, it was unlikely anyone would have noticed them at all unless they saw them in the perfect light at the perfect angle. He took out his paper and pencil and made a careful rubbing, smiling as the symbols reveal themselves. When he had finished, he took out his pocketknife and gently scraped the surface until the symbols were no longer visible. It was a dick move, but treasure-hunting was a dangerous game and if it would keep the Knights of the Golden Circle off his ass, that was fine by him.

"What did you find?" Kendra said as he hopped to the ground

"I'm not sure. We'll know as soon as we decipher the codes on the map."

12

Stetson Rice knelt before his makeshift altar and prayed for peace. Not peace for the world, peace for himself. It had been a long couple of days and disposing of Austin's body and his vehicle had been an annoyance he didn't need. He was looking forward to catching a few hours of shuteye.

He had just laid down on his cot when Colt called. Colt was one of the Galveston lot, a bottom-feeder. Rice's stomach sank. If the man was calling him directly, it wouldn't be good news.

"What's the situation?" he snapped.

"There's good news and there's bad news," Colt said. "Which one do you want first?"

"Bad news. Always the bad news first."

"Well, one of us is dead, another in jail, the third in the hospital in police custody." He went on to spend a ridiculous tale of a scooter and tour boat chase down Seawall Boulevard and a gunfight in the middle of the tourist district.

"Idiots," Rice snapped. "I ordered you all not to engage unless you had acquired the map."

"I know," Colt said. "But Remington and Wesson, they've got a bit of a wild streak in them. One of them yelled, 'Remember the Alamo!' and they just went haring off, guns blazing. Now Remi's dead and Wes is in the hospital."

"Have we been exposed?" Rice demanded.

"No. The authorities think it's just the usual. White men snapping and shooting up a public place. Nothing out of the ordinary."

"Lucky for us." Rice's sardonic reply went right over Colt's head. "You said we had a third in jail. How did Smith end up in custody?"

"It was just dumb luck. We were staking out the Indian's truck. I went to take a leak in the graveyard, and as I was coming back, there was a cop there. I heard him tell Smitty they were looking for a weed dealer. Well, I hid in the graveyard because I had some herbage on my person at that time. But it turns out, so did Smitty. Did you know he's on probation?"

"I did not." Rice sat up, rubbed his temples. He was playing high-stakes poker and he had been dealt a handful of jokers and suicide kings. "What's the good news?"

"I kept an eye on the truck, and the Indian finally came back for it. I followed them to the Texas Heroes Monument."

Rice's shoulders sagged. "There's no vault underneath that monument any more than there is Cornwell's. He's just guessing at this point."

"He didn't try to get under it. He did something really weird. He climbed up onto the monument, and he got right up against one of the statues. Pressed his cheek right up against it. Stared for a long time."

"And?" Rice said. His heart raced. The Knights of the Golden Circle were not strictly aware of the operation he'd been running. But these were his men, and this was his purview. And when he succeeded, he would be a legend!

"I heard him say something about the Moody House, and he got really excited. He jumped right down and hurried away."

"The Moody House," Rice breathed. It made sense. The mansion would have been a fitting place to stand guard over the treasure. But if it was there, getting to it would be tricky. "Anything more specific?"

"No. I followed them back to the place they're staying. I was thinking I might climb up and take a peek through the window."

"Don't get yourself seen… or arrested as a peeping Tom."

"I ain't been caught yet." Three seconds of silence followed Colt's inadvertent admission. Finally, he cleared his throat. "When I'm investigating, of course."

"Don't make any mistakes," Rice said, ignoring Colt's lapse. "I want that map. You keep an eye on them. I'll check out the Moody Mansion."

13

"This is driving me nuts." Bones tossed his pencil onto the table, closed his eyes, and let out a groan of frustration. He felt a firm, gentle touch and then Kendra began to knead his shoulders. The tension immediately drained away, and he let out a groan of contentment. "You are talented."

"Thank you. I actually trained as a massage therapist." She kneaded his shoulders and neck, then began to gently massage his scalp with her fingertips. A warm, tingling sensation spread over him. The woman was a wizard!

"You didn't pursue it as a career?" Bones asked, his eyes fluttering shut.

"I did for a little while. But between the clients who were all hands and the ones who kept trying to talk me into giving them a happy ending, I got sick of it." She stopped rubbing his scalp. The unhappy memory had sapped her enthusiasm.

"That sucks," Bones said.

"It does." She fell silent for a moment and then she brightened. "Let's see if we can figure out this code. What have you got so far?"

"Not much." He had done a deep dive into some of his go-to conspiracy theory forums, and while he had not managed to break any of the codes, he had found some tantalizing clues. He even had a few definite matches. "This first line of symbols is a Confederate code. But not the standard one that everybody knows."

"Everybody?" Kendra echoed.

ALAMO GOLD | 96

He chuckled. "Well, everybody who's into this sort of thing."

"What makes you think it's Confederate?" She was rubbing his shoulders again. Bones was a man of few words, but he would talk all night if she kept it up.

"There are a few similarities, and I've got three symbols that are exact matches for the commonly-known Confederate code: A, C, and S. Not sure why they chose to match only those three."

"Maybe CSA for the Confederate States of America?" she offered.

"Good thinking! I like an intelligent woman," Bones said.

"You like any woman." Kendra paused. "You're not even going to bother to deny it?"

"What would be the point?"

"If you don't mind me asking, what is the longest relationship you've been in?"

"There's a girl I've been seeing on and off for about three years." It wasn't exactly the truth. Jessie was his favorite plus-one, but that was a friendship with benefits. He wasn't sure why he felt the need to mislead Kendra. What did he care if she found out he couldn't keep an actual relationship together for more than a couple months?

"How on and off are we talking about?" she pressed.

"Listen, Oprah, can we get back to the code?" He held up the sheet for emphasis. "I also have it on good authority that the second line of code is of Illuminati origin. Well, the person I got the information from is considered an authority within certain circles."

"What's the problem, then?"

"I assigned the letters to the corresponding symbols

in the unknown code at the bottom of the page. But when I try to translate the message from the memorial, it comes out gibberish."

Kendra took the paper from him and held it up, squinting. "Why are you assuming they're all written from A to Z? Wouldn't that make it far too easy for someone who isn't an initiate to decipher the code? If it were me, I'd moved the letters around."

"You mean like a Caesar Shift cipher? That's pretty basic for a secret message." The Caesar Shift was a substitution cipher in which each letter of text was replaced by a letter a fixed number of positions down the alphabet. It was named for Julius Caesar who used it in his written communication.

"But this isn't a message. It's a resource for initiates of one of these secret societies. Whoever made it wouldn't want to make it too convoluted."

"I'll give it a shot. What number should I try first?"

She leaned down for a closer look. Her hair brushed against his cheek, sending a shiver down his spine. Suddenly he was having a tough time keeping his mind on code-breaking.

"Shouldn't you start with one and try them all?"

"You sound like Maddock. That's not my style. I like to start with my best guesses."

"How do you come up with a best guess in this situation?"

"There would usually be a keyword. You'd count the number of letters in the word, and that would be your shift."

"Knights? Golden? Circle? Treasure? Texas?" she offered. "Unless Gonzales arranged these for his own use, in which case he might have used something meaningful only to him." She paused as Bones let out a frustrated growl. "Like I said. Go in order."

"Screw that. I'll figure it out."

The hour was growing late, and sleep threatened to overtake them. While Kendra made coffee, Bones turned the problem over in his mind. He took out Gonzales' map and looked it over. The symbols at the bottom denoted landmarks, but might there be another layer of meaning hidden there?

There was one thread connecting the tomb with the Texas Heroes Monument—the Alamo. He applied a five-letter shift then transcribed the known letters from the Confederate code to the Illuminati. He was encouraged by the fact that a couple of the symbols he matched up bore some resemblance to one another. He repeated the shift and applied it to the last row of symbols, what he had come to think of as the KGC code, for Knights of the Golden Circle. He compared it to the message from the monument. No joy. Not quite ready to give up yet, he tried a shift to the left, and again with no shift at all. Nothing worked.

"Looks like we need a second word to figure out the third line." He took a gulp of strong, lukewarm black coffee.

"Texas? Bowie?" she suggested.

"Those are five letters, same as Alamo."

"How about Crockett?"

Bones tried an eight-letter shift in both directions. Still no luck. He frowned, staring down at the lines of code. This was a treasure map, so why not a word related to treasure?

"How about..." He tried a four-letter shift to the right without success. He then applied a left shift. Once again, he filled in the letters of the alphabet above what he hoped would be the proper corresponding symbols in the KGC code. By now, he was familiar enough with the message they were attempting to translate that he knew in an instant he finally had it right. A smile spread across his face.

"I've got it!" he said.

"Really?" Kendra said excitedly. "What does the message say?"

"SAN SABA WELL CROCKETT KEY," Bones read.

"What does that mean?"

Bones scratched his head. "It must refer to the San Saba Treasure. It's an obscure legend, and the few versions are inconsistent. Depending on who you listen to, it's either a lost gold mine, silver mine, or treasure cache."

"What about 'Crockett Key?'"

"I'm not sure, but considering the keywords, I think I know where we should go next."

"What were the keywords?"

Bones smiled. "Alamo Gold."

"That's amazing!" Kendra hugged him and planted a kiss on his cheek. "I've always wanted to go to San Antonio!"

"You're coming along?" Bones asked.

"Of course I am. I'm off from work for the next three days and I could extend it if need be. My boss is pretty chill about that kind of stuff."

"What if the Knights of the Golden Circle show up?"

She fixed him with a serious look. "If I meet those guys again, I would much rather face them with you than on my own. You got me into this. It's your job to get me out." She grabbed a backpack from her closet and began stuffing items into it. "I assume we are going to leave right away?"

"Sure," Bones said. He stood, stretched, and yawned. A glance at the graying sky outside told him sunrise would come in a few hours. "I want to get a quick shower first." He flashed her a grin. "I could use somebody to wash my back."

Kendra paused in the middle of packing. She quirked an eyebrow and fixed him with a pitying smile. "Here we are becoming friends, and you have to go and hit on me."

Bones raised his hands and took a step back. "Just extending a no-strings invitation. No pressure. Won't happen again." He took a few steps toward the bathroom door, paused, and turned back. "But it is a standing invitation."

Kendra rolled her eyes and returned to packing. Disappointed, Bones resigned himself to showering alone. He turned the hot water up all the way, then stripped down and unbraided his hair while the water warmed up. Soon, a cloud of steam filled the room. Just the way he liked it.

He stepped into the shower and was immediately pleased to find that the old house had good water pressure. He stood there for a long time, letting the hot stream wash over his tired muscles. This made two nights running with very little sleep. He would need to catch some shut-eye soon, but he wanted to stay ahead of the Knights of the Golden Circle.

He considered what he knew about a potential connection between the San Saba Treasure and the Alamo. It wasn't much. The legend went, Jim Bowie had buried a treasure horde somewhere on the grounds of the Alamo, hoping to keep it out of the hands of Santa Ana and his forces. Because some versions of the San Saba legend included Bowie, the two had become conflated. To his knowledge, no treasure had ever been discovered at the Alamo.

He perked up when he heard the door open. And then the light went out.

"Hello?" he said.

"I decided to take you up on your offer," Kendra said. "No strings!" He heard the scrape of the shower curtain being pulled back, the soft pad of feet behind him.

"What's with no lights?"

"I find that the darkness heightens your other senses." She ran her fingernails down the length of his spine, and he shivered.

"I see what you mean." He turned, wrapped her in a tight embrace, and forgot all about treasure for a while.

14

Colt Ryden clambered up the trellis to the third floor of the old house. He shimmied over onto the roof that covered a second-floor sundeck and crept over to the window. Golden candlelight flickered against the pane. It made him think of treasure.

He peered inside. It was a New Age nightmare of hippy dippy shit. Crystals and candles, stinky oils and Satan stars. He shouldn't have been surprised. In the movies, the Indians were all about smoking their weeds and dancing around fires. Or maybe this was the girl's place.

"Maybe she's a witch."

The Indian and his girl were talking about something. He strained to hear what they were saying but could only make out a few words. It sounded like 'San Saba well Crockett." Colt must have misheard. San Saba was a river west of Austin, but the phrase made no sense.

The Indian went into the bathroom and Colt focused on the girl. She was packing a bag like they were leaving in a hurry. Had they already found the treasure? Impossible. He'd kept an eye on this house all night. So, why was she smiling? Probably about to do some yoga and summon the spirits.

Colt looked around the room and something caught his eye. Lying atop a folding table near the window lay a worn sheet of paper covered with lines and symbols. It was the map! He had to get his hands on it! But how? The Indian could return any second. He was just turning over the problem in his mind when the girl stood and began undressing. Instinctively, Colt grabbed his smartphone and activated the camera, but he stopped himself immediately.

"Dammit, Colt! You can't do that stuff anymore. You're a Knight of the Golden Circle now!" With only a small pang of regret, he turned off the camera and tucked the phone into his pocket. He watched as the girl entered the bathroom and closed the door behind her. A crimson wave of envy washed over him, and a bitter taste filled his mouth. Why couldn't he get a girl like that?

The momentary pang of jealousy vanished in a surge of triumph. It looked as though those two would be busy for a few minutes. That meant the map was unguarded! He tried the window. It wouldn't budge. Colt was momentarily stymied by this simple impediment. He had only planned on spying. He had no tools for breaking in, nor was he armed. His sidearm made for awkward climbing and he tended to bump it against things at inopportune times, so he had left it in his truck.

"What am I going to do?"

Lacking a better idea, he tried the window again and tugged with all his might. It budged an inch, enough for him to work his fingers underneath. He gave it another heave. With a slow shriek of protest, the window slid up.

He froze. Had anyone heard? He waited but all he could hear was the rasp of his own breath and the sound of running water from the shower.

"I'm just gonna go for it."

Colt plunged headfirst through the window. He fell awkwardly and landed with a thud. Still, no one seemed to hear. He scrambled to his feet, hurried over to the map. The moment his fingers closed around it he felt an incredible sense of pride and satisfaction. He had done it!

He held the map up and drank in the sight. In the flickering candlelight it really did look like a treasure map. And he was the one who had recovered it for the Knights of the Golden Circle! Or would he?

"Stetson Rice will probably take all the credit! I ought to go right over his head. This is my chance to move up in the organization!" Of course, he didn't know the names of anyone in the organization who ranked higher than Rice. He would simply have to see to it that he was given his due. But first he had to deal with the two in the bathroom. That had been his orders—do not engage unless you have the map.

Colt turned toward the bathroom door. The water was still running. He would take those two completely by surprise. His hand went to his hip.

"Son of a…" He had momentarily forgotten he wasn't carrying. But he couldn't leave them alive. He looked around for a weapon of some sort. His eyes took in the burning candles and the tapestries, and he had an idea.

First, he moved the bookshelf in front of the door, blocking the exit. Next, he used the candles to ignite the tapestries and curtains. They went up slowly, the flames unimpressive. He made a pile of loose papers in the middle of the floor and set those afire as well. As he cleared the folding table of papers, he came across a souvenir map on which someone had drawn several crisscrossing lines. It could be important, so he tucked it into his breast pocket along with the map. Everything else he added to the fire. The room began to fill with smoke, but the fire wasn't spreading fast enough.

An antique kerosene lamp sat atop a mantle nearby.

He grabbed it, hastily unscrewed the wick from the font, which held the kerosene, then began dousing the walls with fuel oil. The flames suddenly shot up like an inferno. He let out a yelp and lost his grip on the lamp. It hit the floor and shattered, splashing kerosene everywhere.

"Dammit to hell!" he grunted as his pant legs caught fire. He smacked at the flames, trying to suffocate them with his hands, but only succeeding in setting his shirtsleeves aflame.

The room had quickly become an inferno. The walls were ablaze and the fire on the floor had spread. Scorching hot flames reached out for him. Thick smoke filled his lungs, robbing him of breath. His eyes, nose and throat burned.

Colt blinked away the tears that clouded his vision. The window, his only way out, was wreathed in flame by the burning curtains. Having no other choice, he made a run for it and dove headfirst out the window. He half-climbed, half-fell down the trellis. When he hit the ground, he rolled across the lawn, damp with morning dew, until the flames were extinguished. He staggered to his feet, sucked in painful breaths of the cool morning air. Large swathes of his shirt and pants had burned away.

"The map!" He snatched it from the remains of his breast pocket and unfolded it. It was mostly intact, with the edges scorched. But there was something different about it. Symbols had appeared all over the page. He gaped as they faded away.

"What the hell?"

There was no time to ponder this new development. Black smoke roiled and tongues of fire poured out of the upstairs window, licked the eaves. Emergency services might already be on their way, and that would include the cops. Time to make tracks. As he stumbled away in the darkness, he smiled despite the pain from his burns. Rice would not be able to find fault with him this time.

15

Bones was just beginning to really enjoy himself when Kendra stiffened, pushed away. Even in the darkness he could sense that something was wrong. He heard the shower curtain draw back.

"What's the matter?"

"I thought I heard something," she said.

"Want me to check it out?" he asked reluctantly. He really didn't want to interrupt what was turning out to be one of the most enjoyable showers he had had in a long time.

"I'll do it." She stepped out of the shower.

"Can it wait for a few minutes? We were just getting started," he said slyly.

"You'll have to finish yourself," she said.

He heard the door open. Immediately he caught a whiff of acrid smoke. Yellow light flickered from somewhere outside.

"Oh my God! The apartment is on fire!" Kendra flipped on the light, snatched up a towel, and hurried out the door. Bones followed, blinking at the sudden bright light and trying not to be too upset about the interruption. He supposed it had been too good to be true. He, too, grabbed a towel, scooped up his discarded clothing, and hurried out the door.

The apartment was an inferno. The curtains and tapestries were ablaze. There was a pile of papers in the middle of the floor, orange flame and black smoke pouring up from it. Someone had set the blaze intentionally. They tried to fight the fire as best they could, batting at it with towels, dumping half-filled cups of liquid onto the flames, but it was a losing battle.

"We need to get out of here!" he shouted.

Kendra began gathering up items from around the room. Bones turned to the table where they had left the map. It was gone!

"Son of a…"

The heat in the thick smoke that filled the room burned his sinuses and dried out his throat. He tried to call out to Kendra, but his voice was a mere croak. He saw her moving through the cloud of smoke, her arms laden with possessions she had gathered. He reached out and grabbed her.

"I can't tell which way is out," she gasped. She tried to say more but her words ended in a rasping cough.

"I've got you," Bones said. He put his arm around her waist and guided her in the direction of the door. They stopped after only a few steps. The fire barred their way.

"How are we going to get out?" she rasped.

"To the window, to the wall." He scooped her up in his arms and made a run for it. He dashed through a wall of flame. The tendrils seared his skin and the smell of burning hair filled his nostrils. Kendra was coughing and gasping, her head buried in his chest. He ran on instinct, stumbling in the direction where he believed the window lay. He couldn't see anything but smoke and the glow of the fire. He couldn't see anything in here. For all he knew he could be moving in a circle.

And then he smashed into something, heard the shattering of glass, felt sharp pain along his elbow. He had run right into the window and broken it.

"Good enough."

He set Kendra down beside the broken window. His fingers found the sash and he threw the window open. He caught a glimpse of a man running down the street. Was that the arsonist? Hastily, he helped Kendra through. She was carrying so many items that she barely fit.

"What is all that stuff?"

"Things we will need. I didn't get the map though."

"Don't worry about that," he said. He gave her a shove and with a yelp she plunged through the window, and he dived through behind her. The roof was slick, and they skidded along its surface toward the ledge. Rough shingles scoured his exposed flesh, but right now he was more concerned about staying alive.

He hooked his left arm around Kendra's waist and grabbed hold of the rain gutter with his right hand just as they fell over the ledge. Pain stabbed through him as his shoulder threatened to dislodge, but he held on. They hung there, naked, two stories above the ground. Distant sirens blared. Someone had reported the fire.

"This is awkward," Kendra said. "How do we get down?"

With a loud squeal the rain gutter gave way. With a thrill of surprise Bones plunged toward the ground. There was no time to cry out before they crashed into shrubbery. A loud crackling filled his ears. Stabs like a thousand needles pierced his flesh, and the impact knocked the wind out of him. He lay there, gazing up at the sky through watering eyes, catching his breath. He was miserable, but alive!

"Are you all right?" Kendra said.

"I'm cut, scraped, and burned, lying naked in the landscaping," he replied.

"So, just another Tuesday for you?"

"Exactly." With a series of grunts and groans, he climbed out of the shrubs and helped her down. They were just pulling on their clothes when the first responders pulled up to the house. Bathed in flashing blue lights, Bones smiled tentatively and waved to the officers and firefighters, all the while wondering how he was going to talk his way out of this one.

16

The Moody Mansion was a historic building in the heart of old Galveston. It was a thirty-one room Romanesque mansion named for William Moody, an American financier and entrepreneur. Built in 1895, the home was converted into a museum in 1986.

It was well before opening time, but Rice had no trouble bribing a security guard to let him in and show him around before anyone else arrived. But after thoroughly inspecting all three floors, including the archives, he had found nothing. He was beginning to think this was a dead-end.

"Were there any legends associated with this house? Mysteries?" he asked, staring out the third-floor window in the direction the Texas Heroes Monument.

"Mysteries?" The guard, a burly young man with a thin ginger beard, scratched his chin and frowned. "There are ghost stories. Visitors report hearing a woman's voice whispering to them. A lot of people say that ghosts show up in their photos. Is that what you mean?"

"Something like that," Rice said, turning away from the window. "How did the Moodys make their fortune?"

"Cotton," the guard said. "Same as the family who originally owned it."

"No buried treasure then?" Rice forced a laugh.

"None that I've heard of. I guess you could check out the basement."

"Basement?" Rice perked up. "I definitely want to see that. Lead the way."

The basement was a disappointment. Although the Moody mansion had avoided damage from the great hurricane of 1900, Hurricane Ike in 2008 had caused significant damage, including flooding the basement, kitchen, servant's quarters, and potting room. In the aftermath, the city renovated the basement and converted it to a children's museum. Rice gave the area a thorough inspection but saw nothing to indicate that treasure had ever been hidden here.

He had just made up his mind to leave when he heard footsteps coming down the stairs. That was odd. It was still well before the time employees should be arriving.

"Wonder who that is," the guard mumbled, his hand moving to his sidearm.

A few seconds later, Colt appeared in the doorway. There were dark circles under his eyes, but his grin stretched from ear to ear. Rice tensed. Colt was supposed to be keeping an eye on Bonebrake. The man had better have a good reason for his sudden appearance.

"I've got it!" Colt proclaimed. He held up what could only be Gonzales' treasure map.

"What is that?" the guard asked curiously.

Colt blanched, then his face reddened. He had not noticed that the other man was there. Rice's eyes immediately went to the guard's sidearm. The young man was oblivious to the danger he was in. Rice could easily snatch the man's firearm, eliminate him, and cover up the killing. But that would open up a new can of worms.

"It's a map I made of some of the important sites of old Galveston," Rice invented. "I'm writing a book and I thought I had lost this."

Heart racing, he took the map from Colt. He wanted to pore over it right then, but he resisted the urge. He carefully folded it and tucked it into his pocket.

"What's this book about?" the guard said

"Mysteries," Colt blurted.

Rice gritted his teeth. When would Colt learn to keep his mouth shut?

The guard's eyebrows sprang up like a couple of Baptist teenagers caught *in flagrante* on the family sofa. "You mean like the ghost stories?"

"That's it exactly," Rice said. "You were a great help today. I'll bring you a copy of the book when it comes out."

"Will there be a movie?" the guard asked hopefully.

Rice forced a smile through gritted teeth. He was, in fact, a writer and that was always the first question anyone asked when the subject came up.

"Hopefully," he said. "By the way, I would appreciate it if you would not mention to anyone that we were here. I don't want my competitors knowing what I'm working on." A couple of Ben Franklins pressed into the guard's palm sealed the deal.

They drove to a secluded area and parked. Rice took out the map and examined it carefully. There were wavy lines in the center, like channels of a river or underground passageways. A line of symbols ran across the bottom. He immediately recognized one as corresponding to the Cornwell gravesite.

"I guess we will need to identify all the symbols," he said.

"Way ahead of you." Colt took another paper out of his pocket and unfolded it. It was a souvenir map of Galveston. Someone had marked all over it, making dots at various locations, then joining them with a series of straight lines that all met in a single spot near the center of town. "That's the Texas Heroes Monument, where I spied on the Indian last night." He tapped the spot at the center.

"We've got the map but the Indian's ahead of us," Rice said.

"But there's more," Colt said. He took out a cigarette lighter and handed it to Rice. "Hold the flame close to the paper and see what happens."

Rice disliked being led around by the nose, but curiosity and excitement tempered his ire. He did as instructed and smiled as symbols began to appear on the page. It was a code written in invisible ink!

"How did you discover these?" he asked.

"By accident." Colt's cheeks reddened. He went on to describe how he had followed the Indian and the girl back to an apartment. When they had left the map unguarded, he had stolen it and set the apartment on fire.

"So, they're dead?"

Colt shrugged. "Beats me. I didn't go back to check."

"I'm surprised you didn't try to leverage this into a better position among the Knights," Rice said. He could tell by the way Colt momentarily averted his eyes that the man had at least considered it. Rice chose to let it pass. He was fast running out of resources, and he might need Colt before this was all over. Rice could kill him later if need be.

"No, I'm loyal," Colt mumbled.

And you don't know anyone else in the organization who isn't dead or in jail, Rice thought.

"Did you find anything else that might be useful?"

Colt shook his head. "The fire spread pretty quick. I burned my elbow." He turned his arm to reveal an angry red circle. On impulse, Rice slapped the spot with all his might and Colt let out a yelp. "What was that for?"

"I need you to focus and stop worrying about tiny little burns. Now, think hard. Did you hear or see anything that would help us decipher this code?" He tapped the map although the symbols written in invisible ink had already faded away.

Colt's brow furrowed. He scratched his chin and slowly shook his head. Rice's heart fell. They had on this map what looked like three different codes and none of them looked like any he had seen before. If they couldn't decipher the symbols, they were stuck. And then Colt's expression brightened.

"I did hear one thing, but it didn't make any sense. What was it?" As he thought, his eyes narrowed, and his expression twisted into a pained grimace like a schoolteacher on the last day of summer vacation. "It was something like 'San Saba well Crockett.' I can't have heard it right, though. It's just gibberish."

A dagger of fear and anger pierced Rice's chest. He seized Colt's collar and twisted it tight until his face was the color of a Schrute Farms beet. Colt didn't fight back. He stared at Rice through wide eyes.

"Say it again," Rice demanded.

"Can't... breathe," Colt wheezed. It took Rice a moment to regain control of himself. He loosened his grip on the man's throat. Colt gasped, sucked in ragged breaths. When he could once again draw breath, he repeated what he had heard.

Rice's head spun. He knew the legend of the San Saba treasure but had always considered it highly unlikely. There was not a shred of documentation to support the notion that there had ever been treasure in the Alamo. Furthermore, the legend was little-known and short on details. And then Gonzales and his brother had come along and stirred the anthill. How Bonebrake had come to be involved he had no idea.

"What does it mean?" Colt asked. "Did Davy Crockett hide treasure in a well near the San Saba? Is this the 'Texas Treasure' Austin was always talking about?"

"David Crockett did not bury anything anywhere," he replied sourly as he shifted the vehicle into gear and merged into the light early morning traffic. "Texas Treasure" was a term Rice himself had invented to keep his underlings from knowing what he was actually searching for.

"Who is David Crockett?"

"Crockett never went by Davy. That was a nickname others called him."

"Austin said the treasure..."

"Austin talked too much," Rice snapped. "And now he's dead. Take a lesson from that."

Colt paled and he lowered his gaze to the floorboard. After a few minutes of blessed silence, he finally summoned the courage to speak again.

"Where are we going?" he asked.

Rice merely frowned and kept driving. He had too much on his mind to bother with answering questions. The discovery of the San Saba treasure could be a boon to Texas, a source of pride and a unifying force in a fragmented time. But if Crockett were involved, it was imperative that he get there first. If not, the consequences could be devastating.

17

The Alamo was a historic Spanish mission built in the eighteenth century by Roman Catholic missionaries in what was now the heart of San Antonio. Also designed to serve as a fortress, the compound consisted of a few buildings surrounded by a stone wall. It was on this site that the famed Battle of the Alamo took place in 1836. The heroic last stand made by the defenders, who were outnumbered almost ten to one, inspired Texas revolutionaries in their fight against Mexico. It was considered a seminal event in Texas history and had spawned many heroic legends and inspired a popular film starring John Wayne.

"I didn't realize that it was right smack in the middle of the city," Kendra said as they followed the signs toward the entrance. "It kind of takes away from the mystique." The city encroached on all sides, depriving the old battlefield of much of its historical charm.

"You should see the pyramids in Egypt," Bones said. "Look to the West, pyramids. Look to the right, Walmart. Well, maybe not at Walmart, but you can see the Marriott from the top of the Great Pyramid."

"You've been atop the great pyramid?"

"I've been on top of all sorts of things I'm not supposed to." He winked, but she met him with a blank stare.

"You are gross," she said.

It had already been another tiring day. The firefighters on the scene had declared the fire at Kendra's apartment an act of arson, although theirs was not the final word. Luckily, both the first responders and Kendra's landlord had seen a man fleeing the scene. This allowed them to offer a version of the truth, that a burglar or maybe a jealous ex-boyfriend, had set the fire. Given that Kendra owned nothing of real value—save her ghost hunting equipment, which had survived the blaze—it was obvious she had no motive for setting the fire. As soon as they were able, they had made the four-hour drive from Galveston to San Antonio, arriving at the Alamo a couple of hours before closing time.

They purchased tickets and joined the tour that was about to start. Their guide was a man named Kenneth. He looked to be in his late twenties, but already his blonde hair was thinning on top. He wore John Lennon glasses which were apparently for show because he removed them whenever he needed to read something.

Kenneth proved to be an entertaining and knowledgeable guide. He had a wealth of knowledge about the battle and those who participated, and he sprinkled in interesting details and anecdotes at each stop on the tour. The original grounds covered three acres and was surrounded by a ten-foot-high adobe wall. The inside of the fort included a chapel, a barracks for soldiers, a hospital room, a large courtyard, and a horse corral. Cannons were set along the walls and atop buildings. Unfortunately, the fort had been designed to hold off lightly armed natives, and not a modern army with heavy artillery, which made the task faced by the defenders all the more daunting. Tourists nodded along as Kenneth described acts of valor by the defenders.

"Sadly, the Battle of the Alamo should never have happened," Kenneth said. This elicited confused murmurs. "At the time of the Texas Revolution, this place was a long way from the east Texas cities populated by Americans, and quite close to large Mexican settlements. It was of no strategic importance to the revolutionaries. The defenders were ordered to abandon the Alamo and make a strategic retreat to a more defensible position where they and their cannons could be of greater use. The defenders chose to stay and fight, believing that reinforcements would arrive in time to save the fort. Sadly, they were wrong. Everyone who fought that day lost their lives, but 'Remember the Alamo' became a refrain that helped lead the revolutionaries to victory, and still echoes down through history."

People in the tour group were exchanging uncomfortable looks. A few asked questions that were obviously meant to discern on which side of the political fence Kenneth stood. Bones rolled his eyes. He was fed up with assclowns for whom the only measures of truth were the politics of the messenger and whether or not the message agreed with their existing beliefs. Things like objective facts were fast becoming artifacts of a bygone era.

"Imagine, if you will, a place where people who are not citizens are taking over," Kenneth began. "They immigrate in droves until they vastly outnumber the citizens. They work hard, but they don't pay taxes, they buy their goods from across the border instead of at home, and they don't follow the laws."

Tension immediately stretched over the assembled tourists. Bones thought he saw a twinkle in Kenneth's eye, as if the guide took pleasure in antagonizing his guests. What was the man up to?

"Suppose the government placed tariffs on these

foreign goods, and tried to enforce the rule of law, but these non-citizens refused to comply."

"Can we not get political?" a young woman grumbled. Several voices were raised in assent, while others urged Kenneth to continue. Bones sensed a twist coming.

"Oh, you thought I was talking about today?" Kenneth said in mock surprise. "I'm talking about the people who fought the Texas Revolution. They didn't want to pay taxes, didn't want to pay tariffs on American goods, and continued to keep people enslaved even though slavery was illegal in Mexico and its territories. Santa Ana cracked down hard on them, too hard according to most scholars, and it led to a revolt."

"That's not true!" someone shouted.

"Santa Ana unilaterally revoked Mexico's constitution and ruled as an authoritarian!" a second tourist chimed in.

Bones sensed that things were about to get out of hand. He summoned his best command voice and thundered, "Where did Ozzy take a leak?" Silence and then peals of laughter from the tour group.

"That is a quite a story!" Kenneth said. "Back in 1982, rock singer Ozzy Osbourne had been partying a bit too hard at a nearby hotel and decided he wanted to take a walk. His wife-to-be had hidden all his clothes, hoping that would keep him from leaving their suite. Unfortunately, she left her own clothing behind. Ozzy donned one of her dresses and wandered drunkenly out onto the street." The tension gradually dissipated as Kenneth described an intoxicated and thoroughly befuddled Osbourne searching for somewhere to empty his bladder. Coming across what he believed to be an ordinary wall, Ozzy ended up watering the memorial cenotaph outside the grounds. He was subsequently banned from playing San Antonio again until ten years later, when he publicly apologized and made a donation to the organization that maintained the Alamo grounds. "I think we can all agree that, although he did not foul the Alamo itself, the act was disrespectful," Kenneth concluded. This proclamation seemed to bring the group together again.

Bones shrugged. He didn't disagree, he simply found it sad that folks these days could summon such passion for symbols of their nation while caring very little for the actual people who comprised that nation.

Kenneth steered away from more controversial proclamations as he guided them through the mission building. It was smaller than Bones had expected, only sixty-three feet wide and thirty feet tall according to their guide. After the battle, the Alamo had been utilized by a variety of groups and many had left their marks. Archaeologists studying the old fort had uncovered graffiti left by soldiers, even bits of Confederate code, which Bones found particularly interesting.

"Where did Davy Crockett die?" someone asked as the tour was wrapping up.

"No one knows for certain," Kenneth explained. "Some say he died fighting out in the yard. Others say he surrendered after being overwhelmed by sheer numbers and was later executed. The bodies of the combatants were burned and buried somewhere in the area, but they haven't been found."

"Crockett did not surrender!" one of the tourists piped up angrily. "Everybody knows he fought to the death."

"Either he fought to the death, or he fought until he was as good as dead," Bones said. "Either way he showed courage and died for the cause."

"Unless," Kenneth said, raising a finger like a professor making a crucial point, "you believe the legend that Crockett did not die at the Alamo."

Bones and Kendra exchanged glances. Might this be connected to the mystery of the treasure?

"I've never heard that story," Bones said.

"And you never will!" a voice said from behind them. A burly man in a tour guide's uniform seized Kenneth by the arm and steered him away from the group. "I told you there's no place for your revisionist history here. You're fired!"

"Wait until my book comes out," Kenneth shot back. "Everybody is going to know the truth! Then you'll owe me an apology."

"The only apology I owe is to these people here who had to listen to you cast aspersions against a true hero." Some of the tourists applauded and whistled. Others merely shrugged and drifted away. "Get out of here!" The man pointed in the direction of the front door.

"I guess that's the end of our tour," Kendra said. "This was a dead end."

"Maybe not," Bones said. "I'd like to have a talk with Kenneth."

They found the tour guide sitting on the ground near an old well. He cast a surprised glance at the two of them as they approached.

"If you want your money back, you'll have to talk to the ticket office," he said.

"Not at all," Bones said. He took a seat on one side of Kenneth and Kendra the other. "It was a good tour. I'm sorry you got fired."

Kenneth smiled. "My boss has fired me three times already. He hates my alternative facts, but he hates hard work even more. He's too lazy to file my paperwork much less look for someone else who knows half as much about local history as I do. He fires me for show so the tourists don't complain. My job is safe."

"Has anyone ever caught on?" Kendra asked.

Kenneth shook his head. "This is such a small place that most people don't visit more than once." He sat up a bit straighter. "How can I help the two of you?"

"We were wondering if you had some more little-known legends you could share with us," Bones said.

Kenneth quirked an eyebrow. "Such as?"

"Any treasure stories?" Kendra's face immediately turned a delicate shade of pink.

Bones winced. Had she said too much too soon? Kenneth was unfazed.

"There is a legend that the defenders of the Alamo buried treasure at the bottom of a well to hide it from Santa Ana."

"Maybe it's the bottom of this well?" Kendra asked, pointing at the old well against which Kenneth reclined.

"It was excavated long ago," Kenneth said. "Besides, it does not appear on any of the historical documents that show the layout of the Alamo at the time of the battle. There is a spot under the main walkway where a well existed at the time of the battle. When it was excavated, they found historical artifacts, but no treasure."

"You really know your stuff," Bones said admiringly.

Kenneth shrugged. "I'm an author. I'm working on a book that tells the whole truth about the Alamo, not just the heroic legends. The little-known stuff, the things the powers-that-be want to suppress."

"That's right up my alley," Bones said. "I look forward to reading it."

"You can read?" Kendra asked.

"Sure I can, as long as there are pictures." Bones flashed a smile in Kenneth's direction. "Are there pictures?"

Kenneth chuckled. "Unfortunately, I haven't found a publisher or even an agent yet. They all think my work is too controversial and that I need more *supporting evidence.*" He bracketed the last word in finger quotes and made a face. "But when it's published, yes, I've collected many old photographs, maps, and documents which I hope to include."

"You alluded to a legend that Crockett did not die here. Is that the kind of thing you include in your book?" Kendra asked.

"Exactly," Kenneth said. "I've found all sorts of anecdotes that suggest the history we know isn't what we've been taught. But the publishers all want *proof.*" He scowled, shook his head.

"Can you tell us about the Crockett legend?" Kendra said.

"Some people believe Crockett escaped prior to the battle and lived out the rest of his life in seclusion."

"That doesn't seem consistent with his character," Kendra said. "He was known to be a courageous man."

"It wasn't out of fear. He did it to save the life of the woman he loved. Shortly before the battle, a man standing guard at night was surprised to see Crockett and a woman approach. Crockett handed him a message and then the pair slipped away."

Bones thought he heard a note of disapproval in the man's voice. This was more than a scholarly pursuit for Kenneth.

"It wasn't like he could ever go back East," Bones said. "Crockett ruined his political career when he publicly opposed the Indian Removal Act. Andrew Jackson marked him as an enemy." Bones was not a history nerd like his friend Dane Maddock, but this was a story he knew well, because it hit home to a Native American. An angry Crockett had left his home state, declaring, "You can all go to hell, I will go to Texas."

"What did the message say?" Kendra asked

"'Build an altar of stones from the Alamo so that this will never be forgotten,'" Kenneth quoted automatically.

"I've never heard that story," Bones said.

"It's not very well known," Kenneth said.

"Was such an altar built?" Bones asked.

Kenneth shrugged.

"Have you seen anything on the grounds that could fit the bill? Maybe somewhere underground?" Kendra asked.

"No."

Bones could tell by the way Kenneth averted his eyes that the man was hiding something. Probably holding it back for his book. But they would have to gain his trust if they were to get the truth from him.

"You have probably guessed we're treasure hunters," Bones said. "Maybe we can help one another, share what we know. Finding the San Saba treasure could give you the credibility you need to get published. You'd become an authority overnight."

Kenneth nodded thoughtfully.

"We found an encrypted message on a monument in

Galveston." Bones took out his phone and showed Kenneth a snapshot of the rubbing he had made of the engraving on the Texas Heroes Monument.

"What sort of code is that? Confederate?" His eyes were like saucers. This code was significant to him.

"We think it's the Knights of the Golden Circle. Ever heard of them?" Bones asked, putting his phone away.

"Of course. The Knights had a strong presence among the Confederates who were stationed here during the war." He paused, scratched his chin. "Have you translated the message?"

"It reads *San Saba Well Crockett.*"

"There's a connection between Crockett and the treasure?" Kenneth whistled. "That *would* make an excellent addition to my book." He stood up looked around nervously, brushed blades of grass from his pants. "I can help you. But we will have to come back after hours."

18

It was after midnight when they returned to the Alamo. Bones was pleased that instead of disabling the security system and picking the lock like he would normally have to do in situations like this, Kenneth was able to simply let them in. He wondered about the security guard, but they found the man fast asleep in his golf cart.

"I brought him his favorite macchiato," Kenneth said quietly. "I added a little bit extra to it. He'll sleep for a while, but all we really need to do is get inside. Even when he's awake, all he ever does is drive the perimeter. Never comes inside."

Once inside the mission building, Kenneth led them through arched wooden doors and into the chapel. They followed him into a sacristy. Kenneth pointed to a spot in the corner.

"This niche used to house a statue. The Spanish destroyed it, leaving only the foundation." He indicated a flagstone sitting nearby. "It was recently moved. Underneath it, they found this oversized flagstone covering a secret room."

Bones removed the flagstone and shone his light inside. The beam fell upon skeletal remains lying beside a stone block.

"Who are they?" Kendra asked.

"A woman, a teenager, and an infant. Archaeologists haven't identified them."

"It reminds me of the bas relief on the Texas Heroes Monument. The part of the Alamo battle scene where Jim Bowie was protecting a woman and her children," Kendra said.

"That looks like a rock from one of the walls outside," Bones said, shining his light on the stone beside the human remains.

"It is," Kenneth said. "If you look closely, you can see bits of wax on top of it. One of the archaeologists who examined the space guessed that this woman and her two children took refuge here during the battle and they simply used that block as a place to set their candles. But it's possible they were using it as an altar."

"What is this place, anyway?" Kendra's voice was filled with wonder and trepidation.

"Frontier missions like this one often included a bolt hole for the clergy in the event of an attack by the natives. No offense," he added with a nervous glance toward Bones.

"None taken," Bones said. "I think we need a closer look." He dropped down into the hidden chamber. He turned to help Kendra, but she playfully shoved his hand away and jumped nimbly down.

"I'm not completely helpless," she said, winking slyly.

They knelt before the altar and gave it a thorough inspection. Bones ran his fingers over the cold, rough stone. He neither saw nor felt anything. They searched the remainder of the room then carefully inspected the skeletal remains without touching them.

"Were any artifacts found with the remains?"

"Everything was left in-situ," Kenneth said. "Do you know what you're looking for?"

"I'm not sure. A map, a code, something that looks out of place?"

"Well, that's obvious," Kendra said. "Someone brought this stone here and mortared it to the floor.

Why do that if it's just something to rest a candle on?"

"Good point." Bones returned to the small altar, grabbed hold of it and gave it a hard shove. It wiggled. He pushed harder and the mortar at the base cracked.

"What are you doing?" Kenneth said. "You shouldn't be messing with that."

"I promise you I'll put it back where I found it." He wrapped his arms around the stone and gave it a twist. It broke free. He set it to the side and shone his light on the spot where it had rested.

"What do you see?" Kendra asked, leaning in so they were cheek to cheek.

"Not a damn thing." Indeed, there was nothing to see except the stone floor. "Weird that somebody took the time to cement it into place. Unless…" He returned his attention to the altar stone. He flipped it over and his face split into a wide grin. Carved on the bottom of the stone was a line of code. "Bingo!"

"Hold on! You actually found something?" Kenneth said.

"More of the code I showed you."

"What does it say?" Astonishment dulled Kenneth's voice.

"I can't say for sure until we try to translate it." That was technically true. Bones had not yet committed the Knights' secret code to memory, but he had worked with it enough that he knew all the vowels and several consonants. And he watched enough *Wheel of Fortune* that he was confident he already knew what was written there.

Kenneth spoke up abruptly. "Someone is coming! Must be security. Wait here and keep quiet. I'll put the flagstone back so he doesn't see."

They heard a small thump and then a scraping sound as he slid flagstone back into place. Then a rumbling sound like a bowling ball rolling across the ceiling filled the chamber. Seconds later, all was quiet.

"Weird," Bones said. "I thought he said the guard never came inside."

"Do you hear a hissing sound?" Kendra asked. "And what's that smell?"

Bones turned his attention from the altar stone. From the far corner, a cloud of gas was pouring from a tiny canister. A minty smell filled his nostrils.

"It's some kind of gas bomb! Try not to breathe!"

Holding his breath, he moved to the trapdoor and pushed it up. It wouldn't budge. What the hell? He tried again, but he couldn't move it. They were trapped!

"What's going on?" Kendra gasped, covering her mouth and nostrils with the front of her shirt.

"I think Kenneth pushed the base of the statue back over the trapdoor. He must be stronger than he looks."

He took off his backpack, which held only a notepad and a few bottles of water, shoved the canister inside, and zipped the pack. It didn't completely seal off the gas, but it might buy them some time. He and Kendra tried to budge the trapdoor, but their combined strength wasn't enough to move it even an inch. They needed another way out.

A thick fog was rising around them, filling the air with a harsh, minty smell. Bones tried not to breath it in, but each inhalation brought stabs of pain to his throat and nostrils. He thought hard. If this were a typical bolt hole for the clergy, there would usually be a way out. But he had seen no sign of a hidden doorway. That left one possibility.

"Check the floor for hollow spaces underneath," he told Kendra.

Like pearl divers, they sucked in deep breaths and plunged beneath the cloud of mist. He put his ear to the floor and rapped on the stone. It was solid. He checked each stone with no success. He was beginning to feel dizzy. There was little time left before the gas overcame them.

"I hope it's knockout gas and not poison," Kendra said.

"Cheerful thought."

His numb fingers slid across the smooth, dry floor, seeming to suck in the cold from the flagstone floor. He felt like he was moving in slow motion. He wobbled to his feet, sucked in another breath, and felt the telltale burn of the gas, which had almost filled the entire space.

He ducked back down and continued his search. As a diver he could hold his breath longer than the average person, but there were limits. He pressed his ear to the stone and was nearly overwhelmed by a wave of drowsiness. He was so sleepy.

And then he heard the telltale hollow sound that indicated there was open space beneath the floor. His thoughts were muzzy, and he wondered if he had imagined it. He rapped on the floor and heard it again.

"Over here!" he rasped.

Kendra crawled over to him, and they tried to work the stone free, but it was stuck tighter than a camel's ass in a sandstorm. He saw no handhold or release lever that would open a trapdoor. Kendra's lips moved but she could not manage the words. She swayed and nearly fell.

"It's now or never," he told himself. His eyes fell on the altar stone, and he had an idea. He picked it up, raised it high overhead and brought it crashing down on the flagstone. It made a pleasant cracking sound. He raised the stone and brought it down again with all his might. Cracks appeared in the floor. "One more time."

He put all his might into the effort. The stone shattered. Mortar crumbled. And then the entire section of floor collapsed, and they plummeted into darkness.

19

Bones let out a surprised shout as he fell. Moments later, he plunged into icy water. He came up coughing and choking, his throat still raw from the gas. He treaded water, looked for Kendra, who surfaced a moment later. She spat out a mouthful of foul water and gagged. Bones helped her swim to a nearby ledge where she sat coughing and retching.

"Disgusting," she finally said. "Did I just drink sewage?"

"Could be water leaking in from storm drains," Bones said, pointing to a crack in the wall where a trickle of water traced a faint trail. He stood, knuckled his back, and shone his light up at the spot from which they had fallen. Rusted iron rings ran down the wall to the ledge where they stood.

"Could this be the well where the treasure is hidden?" Kendra clambered to her feet, suddenly excited.

"Looks more like a passageway than a well," he said, looking all around.

"Oh God, we lost the altar stone!" she gasped.

"It's cool. I already know what it says."

"Are you going to tell me or keep me in suspense?"

"A Bible verse. 'Jesus came to a city called Sychar.'"

"What does that mean?

"Your guess is as good as mine." As his eyes searched the underground chamber, something on the opposite side caught his eye. The top of an arched doorway peeked up above the surface of the water. "And there's the exit."

"What if it's completely submerged?" she asked.

"Then we'll have to come up with another plan."

As they swam across the pool, Bones shone his light down into the water. A narrow walkway ran along the near wall, leading to the submerged doorway on the opposite side. The water was surprisingly deep. There must have been a natural pool here when the room was constructed, and subsequent flooding had raised the water level. The bottom was clogged with muck and debris. As he looked around the dark depths, his light fell on a series of seven identical, zig-zag lines carved on the wall. He had seen similar markings before, but on the other side of the world.

They swam into the flooded passageway. The water was murky, and visibility limited, and a gentle current pushed against them. After a short swim, they came to a stone wall. Clean water poured through cracks at the base, stirring up the silt that covered the floor. It was a strong flow of water, possibly from the nearby San Antonio River. They broke the surface at the mouth of another tunnel. To their left, a gaping hole in the wall opened into a storm drain. In the distance, a glimmer of sunlight shone down from above.

"That looks like a way out," Kendra panted as she hauled herself out of the water. She was dripping wet, and her shorts and t-shirt clung to her body in a pleasing way. She caught him looking and rolled her eyes. "Can we focus here?"

"I'm focused, just not on the mission at the moment."

"That deep pool we swam across, you don't think that's the well, do you?" she said, ignoring his wisecrack. "Because if the treasure is down there it's going to be a pain in the ass to get it out."

"I don't think so," he said, wringing the water out of his long hair.

"What's up with those zigzag carvings on the wall? Another code?"

"An ancient Egyptian ceremonial pool was always rectangular with seven zigzag lines within it. Secret societies love to adopt Egyptian symbols."

"Which means this was more than an escape route for the missionaries," she said.

"Fingers crossed."

The corridor curved to the right, terminating at a deep shaft lined with stone. They shone their lights down and saw a glimmer of shiny metal about twenty feet below. Bones' heart raced. Was this it?

"It's an underground well!" Kendra said. "No wonder it hasn't been found." She cast a nervous glance at Bones. "Do you think that's treasure down there?"

"Only one way to find out."

It was a precarious descent. The stones that lined the well were loose and made for uncertain footing. Twice, Bones nearly fell when a foothold failed to support his bulk.

"I thought you were good at climbing," Kendra said.

"It's not a matter of skill, it's a matter of…" The rock Bones was holding onto came free, and then he lost his foothold. He managed to let out a curse before he hit the ground hard. His knees buckled as pain lanced up his spine. He staggered, tripped over something, and landed face first in the soft earth. Kendra appeared at his side moments later.

"Are you all right?" Concern marred her lovely face.

"I think I hurt my pride more than my body," he

grunted as he climbed to his feet. "But if we find the treasure, it will be worth it."

The glimmer of gold they had spotted from above proved to be the brass binding of an old chest. Excited, they began to dig in the soft earth.

"I found something!" Kendra held up a gold coin. On the obverse side was the image of Lady Liberty wearing a Phrygian cap. An eagle was engraved on the reverse side. The coin was dated 1797.

"That's an American Half Eagle," Bones said. "It's almost pure gold. Keep digging." Minutes later Bones found a silver Spanish real. Dizzy with anticipation, he furiously burrowed through the earth, searching for more treasure. But it was not to be. They found more brass bindings and rotted chunks of wood from old chests, but nothing else of value.

"I can't believe it," Kendra said. "Obviously the treasure was here, but someone must have gotten to it first."

"Or the Texans came back after the war and reclaimed it." Bitter disappointment dripped from his words. "I'm really sorry. I almost got you killed three times and for what? A gold coin worth maybe five hundred bucks? I don't know what the silver is worth, but you can have it, too." He pressed the coin into her hand.

"It's all right." She cupped his cheeks and looked into his eyes. "Crazy as it sounds, I've mostly enjoyed it. Maybe I should give up the reiki and become an adrenaline junkie instead. Race you to the top?"

Bones grinned, but his smile evaporated when his eyes fell on a faint symbol scratched in stone. He moved in for a closer look. His fingers traced two humps joined at the base by a horizontal line.

"More secret codes?" Kendra asked.

"It's called the Djew. It's an Egyptian symbol. Two mountain peaks with the Nile in the middle. It's associated with royal tombs."

"Which were filled with treasure. Nothing like rubbing it in." She punched the stone with the flat of her palm. It slid back with a loud thump. Somewhere inside the walls, a low clacking sound arose. "What just happened? Did I open a trapdoor?" The answer came seconds later when icy cold water cascaded down upon them.

"More like a booby trap," Bones said. "Let's get out of here."

"Not going to happen. Look up there!"

"Holy freaking crap." Through the deluge he could see iron bars blocking their path. There was no way out and the water was rising.

20

Rice and Colt crept up to the door of the Alamo Mission. They paused to make certain no one was looking, then they tried the door. It was unlocked, as had been promised. They found a tall, bespectacled blond man waiting for them. Rice recognized him as Kenneth, an especially knowledgeable tour guide whom he had met a few years ago when he was conducting research about his noble ancestor.

"You said you have information that would be of use to me?" Rice said without preamble.

"Two people showed up today asking questions about the San Sabra treasure and Davy Crockett."

"David Crockett," Rice corrected automatically. "Was it an Indian and a woman?"

Kenneth nodded. "They were asking questions about Crockett and the treasure. They seemed legitimate so I thought you would be interested."

"Where are they now?" Rice's heart raced. The Indian was ahead of him again.

"I showed them to a hidden room, gassed them, and sealed them inside. Then I called you."

"Excellent!" It had been a stroke of good fortune that they had been on the outskirts of San Antonio when Kenneth had finally called him after all these years. "Show me the way."

"Don't forget what you promised. A grand and I get to include any discoveries in my book."

"I forget nothing," Rice says. "First let's see if you can deliver on your promise."

When they opened the trapdoor to the hidden room,

Rice's sense were assaulted by a minty gas that burned his throat. He staggered back, coughing.

"Sorry about that," Kenneth said. "I did tell you I used gas."

Rice ignored him. He peered down through the thinning vapor. The chamber was empty, save for a trio of skeletons lying in the beam of his flashlight. "There's no one here." Icy anger clamped down on his chest.

"That's impossible!" Kenneth knelt by the trapdoor. "And the altar stone is gone, too. What happened?"

"Altar stone? What are you talking about?"

"I told them the story about Crockett escaping with his mistress, leaving a note with instructions to build an altar."

"That's a bullshit myth," Rice growled. "Not one bit of corroboration."

"I immediately thought of this room because there was a stone block inside. I didn't actually believe it was an altar, but I thought it was close enough that I could lure them inside here and trap them until you arrived."

"Are you saying the stone *was* an altar?" Colt piped up.

"A symbolic one, maybe. All I know is there were carved symbol on the underside, a code, I think. But I don't know how they got out."

Rice considered killing Kenneth out of sheer frustration, but he managed to calm himself. The man still might be a useful source of information. He continued to search the room. When the beam of Rice's flashlight reached the far corner, he understood what had happened. What he had taken for deep shadow was in fact a missing section of floor. The trio climbed down for a closer look.

"That's a long drop into some nasty water," Colt said. "I wonder how deep it is?"

"Only one way to find out." Rice pointed down. Colt hesitated. "You don't want to end up like that security guard, do you?"

Colt blanched, shook his head. He took a couple of deep breaths, gathered himself, and jumped in feetfirst.

"What happened to the guard?" Kenneth asked.

"You told me you would take care of him, but he was on patrol when we slipped through the security gate. So, he went for a swim at the River Walk," Rice said.

Kenneth went beet red but kept his silence.

"It's disgusting down here!" Colt shouted.

"Any sign of them?" Rice asked.

"Nope."

"What about the altar stone?" Kenneth gave a brief description.

"Probably took it with them," Colt panted, treading water.

"That would be impossible," Kenneth said. "It would be far too heavy to swim with. It's got to be at the bottom of the pool."

"Dive down and take a look," Rice ordered.

Colt made a face but did what he was told. He resurfaced ten seconds later, gasping for breath.

"There's a thick layer of crap down at the bottom, silt and garbage. Lord knows how deep it goes."

Rice's anger burned white hot. The Indian had the next clue, and the stone was gone. This couldn't be the end of the line. They had to find it.

"I think I see a way out on the other side," Colt called up to them. "Like the top of an arched doorway. Maybe they went through there."

"Go find out!" Rice ordered.

"You know, we might not need the stone," Kenneth said, as Colt swam away.

Rice's temper, always barely in check, flared anew. "I must have it," Rice said. "And Colt could use some help." With that, he shoved the tour guide into the hole.

21

"**What are we** going to do?" Kendra shouted. Icy water spilled down over them, filling the old well. It was already above their waists and rising fast.

"Just keep your head above water while I figure something out. And don't touch anything else."

"You said the Djew symbol represented royal tombs! It made sense!"

"It also symbolizes death and the Nile River. Put them together and you drown."

"You omitted that part."

"I didn't think of it right away." Bones was beginning to understand why Maddock always encouraged caution, and why he got so pissed off when Bones ignored him.

"Do you see any more Egyptian symbols? Like the goddess of shutoff valves?"

"Won't hurt to look. Won't be easy. The one I found was so faint it was almost invisible."

One by one, they inspected the stones, but the falling water and years of accumulated dirt and grime made it difficult. The water had risen to his shoulders now. Kendra, who was several inches shorter, clung to the wall, her head just above water lever. He was shivering from the cold, his fingers were numb, his touch clumsy.

"Maybe we could float up with the water and try to work the bars loose?" she asked.

Bones didn't reply. His searching fingers found a straight line. He followed it, tracing out a shape like a step pyramid. A glimmer of hope flared inside of him.

"It's the Primordial Hill! It represents the moment of creation, when dry land rose from the water."

"How about you push the button first and lecture me later?" she said.

Bones gave the stone a hard shove. It swung back and locked into place. The downpour slowed to a trickle. The iron bars slid back into the wall. There was a loud sucking sound as the water drained from the well, washing away the layer of dirt that covered the bottom. Soon, all that was left were the brass bindings from the old treasure chests and a book-sized marble slab that had been buried beneath the silt.

Kendra picked it up, turned it over, and gasped. Smiling, she held it up for Bones to see. On the back were more words written in Confederate Code.

"I vote we translate it right now. You know, in case we lose this one, too."

"Always the optimist," Bones said. Bones had created a key to decipher the code and had saved it on his waterproof smartphone. He consulted it and quickly decrypted the message.

The key is found on the back of a camel

D Crockett

"Does that mean what I think it means?" Kendra asked.

"I think Crockett did leave before the battle," Bones said. "But it wasn't for a woman. I believe he was tasked with hiding the treasure somewhere Santa Ana would never find it, and he left this clue for the Texans who survived the battle."

"I agree. Now we just need to figure out what it means."

Buoyed by their discovery, they carefully climbed up

out of the well.

"I cannot wait to get back to the hotel and get a nice, hot shower. I smell like a sewer," Kendra said.

"Together again? You know, to conserve water?" Bones asked with a grin and a wink.

"Not after what happened last time."

Bones was trying to come up with a counterpoint when out of the darkness stepped a man holding a gun. His finger was on the trigger, his aim steady.

"I finally got you," the man said. "Now, drop the bag."

22

Rice sat in the escape room entertaining angry thoughts and waiting impatiently for Colt or Kenneth to find something. It was essential that they get to the bottom of this mystery. If Crockett were involved in any way with the treasure of the Alamo, it was essential that Rice know the whole truth. Only then could he determine if he could share it with the world, or permanently suppress it.

He heard a commotion, saw a flicker of light. He peered up out of the chamber. In the adjoining room, blue lights flickered against the walls. The police were on the scene!

"Son of a bitch. How?" Rice struggled to make sense of it. Kenneth would not have double-crossed him. The man was just as embroiled in this as Rice was. "They must have found the security guard's body."

He hastily pulled the flagstone back over the trapdoor leading into the small underground chamber. He could hide down here and hope no one remembered the secret room beneath the sacristy. After a moment of contemplation, he concluded that was a risk he could not take. There was only one way out. He looked at the hole in the floor with distaste. There was no other way.

He spotted a series of rusty iron rungs running down the wall. He climbed down to a narrow ledge. Kenneth had just surfaced and swam over to meet him.

"There's a passageway on the other side of that arch. Colt is checking it out."

Rice's heart raced. Might it lead to the legendary well?

"What about the altar stone?"

"I'm sorry but there's no way in hell we're going to find it. There must be several feet of muck and mire at the bottom of this pool. We'd have to pump the water out, which is probably impossible since the river seems to be feeding it. Then we'd have to excavate by hand.

Rice gritted his teeth, once again suppressing the urge to kill someone. Right now, he needed support more than he needed to vent his rage.

"Do you have anything good to tell me?"

"I was trying to tell you before you shoved me through the hole. I captured some video while they were examining the stone. Just be glad I keep my phone in a waterproof case."

Rice nodded. That was at least cause for hope.

"Can you describe the code?"

"It looked the same as the code they said they discovered on a monument."

Rice's heart raced. This meant Bonebrake was definitely on the right track.

"At first I thought it was a Confederate code, but they said it was a secret code used by the Knights of the Golden Circle. All I know is it looks a hell of a lot like a code that's written in my family Bible."

"Do you have possession of this Bible?" Rice asked.

"Absolutely."

Rice's heart leaped. Finally, something was going his way!

"Kenneth, I think you just might have earned your thousand bucks."

23

This was not the first time Bones had stared down the barrel of a weapon. He was calm, but knew he was in trouble. There was no way he could draw his Glock before the newcomer squeezed the trigger. The man's finger on the trigger made him nervous.

Bones was certain this was the person who had started the fire at Kendra's apartment. That meant he was a Knight of the Golden Circle.

Bones did the only thing he could think of. He contorted his finger to form the odd shape Kendra had taught him, making the distress signal of the Knights of the Golden Circle. The man blinked, took a step back, but he didn't lower his weapon.

"Oh Lord, my God," he said tentatively.

"Is there no help for the widow's son?" Bones replied.

With the ritual complete, the man relaxed a little. "Who the hell are you?"

"You want me to say it out loud? Who do you think I am?" Bones made a show of looking around as if someone might overhear them. "I'm a Knight," he whispered. The man visibly relaxed, but still he kept his weapon held steady. "People call me Bones."

"How come I've never heard of you?"

Bones remembered something Austin had told him about the Knights. Secrecy was paramount and few members knew one another's name.

"Same reason I've never heard of you, I suppose. I only know a couple of names. They mostly keep me in the dark," Bones replied. Kendra nodded, afraid to say anything.

"All right, Bones. I can maybe believe you're a Knight, but a woman?" He scowled at Kendra.

"She's been helping me, but she didn't know anything about who I'm with until you forced me to say it out loud." Bones feigned anger.

"You didn't say the whole thing," the man said, suddenly caught off guard.

"I know nothing, I hear nothing, I remember nothing," Kendra said, playing along. "I don't care if you guys are Knights of the Klan or Knights of the Round Table. I've just been helping my friend with his project."

"Fair enough. My name's Colt."

"Good to meet you," Bones said. "Now that we know we're on the same side can we lower the weapon?"

Colt barked a harsh laugh. "We might be kin but that don't mean we're exactly on the same side."

"What do you mean?"

"You don't work for Stetson Rice, or else you wouldn't be spying on him."

"Why would I be spying on a real estate broker?"

"Nice try. You know I ain't talking about his grandfather. Stetson Rice III. He saw you spying on him at his Crockett shrine."

A shrine devoted to Davy Crockett? Bones thought. No wonder the picture had looked familiar.

"What is that?" Colt asked, noticing the marble slab Kendra was holding.

"A souvenir from the gift shop," Bones said.

"Funny guy. Hand it over and maybe I can begin to trust you."

Kendra hesitated, looked at Bones.

"Do it," he said. They had already translated the

artifact, but Colt didn't know that. If turning it over to him would get them out of here alive, that was a trade Bones was willing to make.

She handed Colt the slab. His jaw dropped when he saw the inscription.

"Where did you find this?"

Bones saw no reason to lie. The well wasn't that hard to find. He described the old well and the broken treasure chests at the bottom.

"The only thing left was this stone."

"You expect me to believe that?"

Bones shrugged. "I'm sure you'll check for yourself."

"Damn right I will." He stared in amazement at the inscription. "So the treasure really was buried here. Where did they move it to?"

"I'm sure you'll figure it out. You have Gonzales' map."

Their eyes met. "Yes, I do," Colt said proudly. "Now, get the hell out of here before I change my mind."

Weapon at the ready, he followed them to the tunnel leading up to the storm drain and watched as they climbed up. They emerged on a city street and immediately had to duck back down as a big rig rumbled over them. When it was gone, Bones scrambled out and helped Kendra up.

Nearby at the shore of the Riverwalk, police cars, paramedics, and an ambulance were parked. Lights flashed, sirens blared. A few vehicles slowed for a closer look and were waved away by the officer directing traffic.

"Do you think that has anything to do with us?" Kendra asked.

"I don't know. Just to be safe, we should get out of here." He took her hand and they hurried away.

"What happens now?" she asked.

"It's a race to the finish. First one to figure out the clues wins."

24

Kenneth's heart raced and cold sweat streamed down the back of his neck. It was a sultry night, the moon was full, and a chorus of mosquitoes sung a shrill tune in his ear. So far, treasure hunting wasn't turning out to be the thrilling adventure he had always imagined. It was a dirty, tedious affair, and the company was distinctly unpleasant.

"You mean there's real woolly mammoths in there?"

"Shane, you're an idiot," Colt said.

"I'm just asking. You don't have to be an asshole about it."

Kenneth closed his eyes and tried to wish these two away, but when he opened them again, Colt and Shane were still there. Shane was a new addition to their party, an old friend of Colt. He was big, strong, slightly overweight, and as dumb as the day is long.

"Mammoths have been dead for millions of years," Colt said. "All that they have in there are fossils."

"That's what I meant. Real fossils!"

The Waco Mammoth National Monument was a museum and paleontological site located on the outskirts of Waco, Texas. It was on this site that the fossilized remains of twenty-four mammoths and other mammals from the Pleistocene Epoch had been discovered. The small park was a little-known gem of Central Texas.

"Believe it or not, the last mammoths died out only 3,700 years ago, at a place called Wrangel Island," Kenneth said. "It's funny to think they were still around during the lifetime of someone like Moses or Abraham."

"Lincoln?" Shane cocked his head and frowned.

"Abraham from the Bible, dumbass," Colt said.

Kenneth was beginning to believe Colt had brought in Shane simply because Colt was tired of always being the dumbest person in the room. Idiots or not, they were also dangerous, his alliance with them tenuous.

"I'm not a dumbass," Shane said. "Thomas Jefferson believed there were woolly mammoths living out West when he sent Lewis and Clark on their mission. Ain't that right, Kenneth?"

"They were also looking for Sasquatch," Kenneth said, surprised by Shane's knowledge.

"I heard the Illuminati was involved," Shane added in a whisper.

Yesterday, Kenneth would have mocked him. But today, here he was about to break into a government facility to search for a message written in a secret code.

Truth really is stranger than fiction. The thought made him sick to his stomach. He was betting his career, maybe his life, on that old cliché.

They came to a spot where a gravel road cut through the forest, leading up to a security gate. They waited while Rice disabled the security camera and unlocked the gate. For a self-described scholar and a fellow author, Rice had a surprisingly varied skillset. From there it was a quick jog to the exhibit building where Rice once again made child's play of the security system.

They looked down upon a remarkable sight. Below them lay a prehistoric graveyard! Rather than removing the fossils to a laboratory or museum, the remains had been left in-situ, and the exhibit constructed around it. A walkway ringed one side of the building, allowing visitors to look down upon the site without disturbing it.

His eyes fell upon the partially excavated skull of a bull mammoth. It was massive! A man could have stood in one of its gigantic, curved tusks. The remains of other prehistoric animals were also visible, six in total.

Shane began whistling the Flintstones theme song, prompting Colt to send him outside.

"Stand guard. Let us know if anyone comes this way."

Getting down to the fossils was a matter of hopping two gates and descending a ladder. The site had been designed with ease of access for future study in mind.

"You're sure this is the right place?" Rice snapped. The man had been in a foul mood ever since Kenneth had proven his worth by using the code written in his family Bible to decipher the message Crockett had left in the underground well. But that hadn't earned him any credit with Rice, who seemed upset by Kenneth's success.

"I'm certain that Crockett came across this place on his way to the Alamo. He told the story to a survivor of the battle." Kenneth tried to keep the bitterness from his tone.

"How did he find it if it was buried?" Colt asked.

"The site was partially exposed when modern-day archaeologists discovered it," Kenneth said. "It must have been the same in Crockett's day. He specifically mentioned a giant tusk and a camel. It was fresh in his mind when he reached the Alamo, and anyone to whom he told the story would understand the clue."

"*If* it was even Crockett who left the message." Rice ducked his head and quickened his pace.

"Man, Rice is boiling!" Colt whispered. His grave tone of voice betrayed no awareness of the pun he had made.

"I don't suppose you figured out the message from the altar stone, did you?" Rice called back over his shoulder, condescension dripping from every word.

Kenneth rolled his eyes. The few seconds of video he had captured had been out of focus. He had managed to decipher several letters, but not enough for a breakthrough.

"I gave it Shane to look at," Colt said. "He's good with puzzles."

"Here's the camel," Rice said.

They stood above the fossilized remains of a camel. On a normal day, Kenneth would have been thrilled to experience this up close. Now, he felt sick. This didn't look right at all.

Colt seemed to sense it, too. He glanced nervously at Rice, who had gone silent again.

"Let's give it an up-close look," Kenneth said. "If Crockett scratched a keyword into the exposed stone, it would have been faint. Something a person wouldn't find unless they were actively searching for it."

Rice nodded and they set to work, examining every inch of the camel and the stone in which it was entombed. With each minute that passed, the unease brewing in Kenneth's gut simmered. If he was wrong about this, no telling how Rice would react. The man was not physically intimidating, nor was he particularly bold or aggressive. He was the kind who seethed with silent rage, never showing all his cards. The kind who might not beat you in a fair fight but would shoot you in the back without a second thought.

"There's nothing here," Rice finally said.

Kenneth stood, took a couple of steps back, and let his hand drift toward his pistol, just in case. He held his breath, waiting for whatever came next. Colt seemed to feel the same way. Rice's henchman was inching away.

"It's all right," Rice finally said. "I knew it was a longshot, but I wanted to see for myself, just in case there was something the paleontologists missed."

A wave of relief flooded over Kenneth. He felt like a balloon suddenly deflated. He was a fair shot, but he had never killed anyone. He was almost certain he could do it if it meant past wrongs would be righted.

"What's our next move?" Colt asked.

"I have a pretty good idea about what else the clue might mean. We just need to know where to look."

"Why can't we put what have into a computer and let it figure it out for us? Don't they have an app for that?"

"There are programs we could use if we knew for certain how many words there are in the message and how many letters in each word," Kenneth said. "Which we don't have."

Rice was about to speak when a gunshot rang out. The three men drew their weapons and looked around.

"Sounded like it came from outside," Colt whispered.

A few seconds later, the front door swung open and Shane hurried in.

"Just wanted to let you know there was a guard coming, so I shot him," he said.

"What?" Colt shouted.

"You said to stand guard and tell you if anyone was coming. I stood guard and then I came and told you. The other good news is, I figured out y'all's Bible verse."

"What Bible verse?" Rice said.

"The one from Kenneth's puzzle." Shane strode out

onto the observation deck until he stood directly above them. "You were missing the first word and you didn't have the right number of blanks, but if there's one thing I know, it's puzzles and Bible verses."

"That's two things," Kenneth said.

"Anyhow, I wrote it down." He took out a sheet of paper, crumpled it into a ball, and tossed it down to Kenneth.

"Did you have to crumple it up? You couldn't have made it into a paper airplane or something?" Colt complained.

"My bad. Toss it back up here and I'll make it into a plane for you."

"Forget it," Kenneth said. He unfolded the paper and held it so Rice and Colt could see. There were the symbols he had deciphered.

s ca e t a c t   all d ycha

Below them, Shane had written:

Jesus came to a city called Sychar

"It could be a fit," Kenneth said. "How did you make the connection?"

"I'm the smartest person in my family." He tapped the side of his head. "Also, that verse just came up in our last Christian Lions group outing."

"What are Christian Lions?" Kenneth asked.

"We are a group of believers who understand that, if we want to spread Christ's love, the real world sometimes forces us to resort to any and all means necessary to guarantee our survival."

"So, living according to the Beatitudes would be like opposite day for you guys?" Kenneth deadpanned.

"Whose attitudes?" Shane asked.

"Forget it," Rice said. "Shane, what does this clue

mean?"

Shane smiled. "It means I know exactly where to go next."

25

Jacob's Well was a karstic spring in Wimberly, Texas, an hour's drive north from San Antonio. The mouth of the spring was a popular swimming hole. Its placid blue waters had drawn in travelers and settlers alike, who named it for Jacob's Well in the Bible.

The inscription on the altar stone was a truncated segment of a longer scripture: *Jesus came to a city of Samaria, called Sychar, near the field that Jacob gave to his son Joseph. Jacob's well was there."* The scripture had in turn led to this spring, and the system of natural underwater caves it harbored beneath its deceptively calm waters.

At first, they had doubted the connection, unable to confirm that the name "Jacob's Well" had been in use at the time of the Battle of the Alamo. Further investigation revealed that divers had mapped the two main underwater caverns, and one of them had matched a section of Gonzales' map.

"It's so peaceful here," Kendra said as she and Bones donned their scuba gear and made ready to dive.

"Don't get complacent," Bones said. "Freshwater caves are dangerous."

"You've already given me the lecture," she said. "And this is hardly my first freshwater dive."

"It's going to be pitch black down there. You'll be okay?" Bones asked.

"I'm more concerned that we haven't found the key. You know, the one hidden on the back of a camel."

Bones shrugged. "Our research didn't turn up a

single clue, so I'm going to trust that we'll find it along the way."

"What if we don't?"

"Then the search continues."

The water was a perpetual sixty-eight degrees but to Bones, it felt like being plunged into an ice bath. Tired as he was, the cold jolted him awake, sharpened his senses. He guided them through the larger of the well's two passageways, following the route laid out on the map.

When they came to the spot where the mapped route diverged from their current path, there was no opening to be seen. Finally, Kendra spotted a crack near the base of the wall. A closer look revealed another passageway that had been blocked by falling limestone.

As they cleared enough rubble to swim through, Bones looked nervously around. Limestone was fragile, cave ceilings prone to collapse. Entire chambers could be sealed off without warning. Everything appeared solid. All they could do was keep a close eye out and try not to cause a collapse.

A short distance later they surfaced in a small chamber. From there, they continued on foot, following the map. They found themselves in a jungle of stone. Stalactites hung like giant icicles above their heads. A forest of stalagmites filled the chamber. A trio of pathways diverged, each leading to a different passageway on the room's far side.

Kendra took a step onto the nearest path. A sharp crack rang out and thin lines shot out across the floor like spiderwebs. Bones grabbed her and pulled her back.

"Limestone," he said. "You never know when it's going to collapse."

"That's comforting. How did they carry chests full of

coins and gemstones across it?"

"I think that's what this clue is for." He pointed at the stalagmite that stood a few paces in front of him. A message had been scratched there using the secret code of the Knights of the Golden Circle! Bones quickly tried to decipher it, but the result was gibberish. "It's encrypted."

"Is it another shift cipher?" Kendra asked.

"That's it!" Triumph surged through him. "The key is on the back of a camel! It wasn't a physical key at all. It's the key to deciphering the code! And what's on the back of a camel?"

"A hump?" Kendra said.

"You got it on the first try!" Bones shifted the code four letters to the right, revealing the message.

"The biggest lie ever told about me," he read.

"In this case, 'me' being Davey Crockett." Kendra tilted her head, thinking. "What was a big lie told about him?" She began humming "The Ballad of Davey Crockett."

"A lot of his legendary frontier exploits were exaggerated as a way of boosting his popularity when he ran for office," Bones said. "Cut it out with that song. It's going to get stuck in my head."

"Raised in the woods so he knew every tree," she sang, taunting him.

"Killed him a bear when he was only three," Bones said, half to himself. "Maybe that's it. But if so, what does it mean?"

"That looks like a bear to me." Kendra shone her flashlight at the mouth of the rightmost passageway. Partially obscured from view by the many stone formations, the entrance was guarded by what had once been a stalagmite. Years of erosion and limestone dripping down from above had reshaped it into a rough semblance of a bear's head.

"Looks good to me," Bones said. "Wait here. I'll check it out."

"You're not leaving me behind," she said.

"At least let me make sure the floor will support us."

They stowed their scuba gear and spare packs off to the side. Bones took a deep breath. Gingerly, he took a step along the path to the right. Then another. It held. After a few paces, he was confident that it would hold. Kendra joined him and they made their way along the winding pathway.

They were halfway across when they heard voices. They turned out their flashlights and hid. A beam of light sliced through the darkness, then others joined it. A faint glow filled the chamber.

"Spread out and keep your eyes open for Bonebrake," a voice said.

"Is that Rice?" Kendra whispered.

"Looks like him," Bones said, peering out at the blonde man. Rice was an enigma. They had learned little about him, except that he was an author and a proud descendant of Davey Crockett. "There's Kenneth, the two-faced assclown. And Colt."

"Who is the burly dude?"

"Son of a... That guy was in the bar the night Gonzales was killed. He tried to start a fight with me."

"What do we do?"

"We're sitting ducks if we stay here. Stay low and keep moving."

They began to crawl along the pathway. The limestone was cold beneath his hands, and it crunched and cracked beneath their combined weight. As they crawled along, the Knights continued to inspect the cavern. In the dim light, Bones began to realize just how fragile the cavern floor was. All around them were sinkholes with a long fall to the water far below.

"I see them!" Colt shouted.

Bones and Kendra had no time to react before the cavern was filled with the thunder of gunfire. Bullets zinged all around as Shane joined in, blazing away. A bullet ricocheted past Bones' head and cracked the floor directly in front of him. As the cracks began to spread, he and Kendra hurried on.

Bullets continued to fly. Amidst the chaos, Rice shouted for his men to hold their fire, but the bloodlust had taken what little common sense they might have had. Bullets pinged around the chamber like deadly hornets. A stalactite was knocked free. It smashed a hole in the floor as it came crashing down.

"Spread out! Find them!" Rice shouted.

Footprints clattered on stone. Seconds later, there was a loud crash and a cry of alarm.

"Rice!" Colt shouted. "Where did he go?"

"The floor gave way beneath him, and he fell," Kenneth shouted. "I can't see him."

"One man down." No sooner had Bone said this than he caught a glimpse of Shane off to the right. Shane spotted him and opened fire.

"Get down," Bones said to Kendra, drawing his own weapon and firing two shots. Shane ducked out of the way.

More bullets flew as the other Knights drew a bead on their location. The many stone formations made it difficult to get a clear shot. The Knights closed in, firing away. Bones looked for opportunities, fired judiciously, trying to keep them at bay. There was a flash of movement off to his left. He held his flashlight on top of his weapon, pointed forward. It looked badass in the movies, but in real life, it gave Bones a target. He fired off two shots, heard a grunt of pain.

Colt stumbled back and fell into Kenneth. Kenneth tried to push him aside, but Colt grabbed hold of him and held on. His lips made a silent plea for help. The dying man's weight made Kenneth stumble and the pair hit the ground hard.

"Dammit, Colt," Kenneth muttered, rolling the dying man off him. He sat up and froze. Cracks appeared all around him. "Oh, my God," he whispered. With a series of sharp snaps and pops like firecrackers, the floor fell out from underneath the two knights.

Bones turned to look around for the remaining Knight when something crashed into him. It was Shane. Bones' Glock went flying as he hit the ground and rolled away. He sprang to his feet and delivered a right cross to Shane's temple. Shane took it like a champ and replied with a haymaker that Bones just managed to duck. He snapped two quick jabs, dodged another vicious swing, and landed an uppercut to the chin.

Blood poured from Shane's nose, but he was unfazed. He feinted, then ducked his shoulder and charged like a bull. There was no room on the safe path for Bones to get out of the way. He was knocked back into a stalagmite that toppled and fell. It rolled a few feet, then crashed through the floor.

Bones froze. He was on uncertain footing, with Shane barring his way back to safety. He stole a glance back. Cracks spread out from the hole left by the fallen stalagmite, creeping ever closer. He had only seconds before the world fell out from under him.

26

Smiling, fists raised, Shane beckoned for him to come on. And then his eyes rolled back and he collapsed in a heap. Kendra stood behind him, holding her spare oxygen canister.

Bones made a run for it. He was almost there. With a sound like thunder, the floor around him came apart. He leaped, hit the ground with a painful thud. He had a moment to reach for Kendra's hand, and then there was nothing underneath him. The world seemed to slow down. Shane's body plunged into darkness. Kendra's hands closed around Bones' wrist. He caught hold of the ledge with his free hand. Jagged stone pierced his flesh but he held on.

It was enough. Kendra helped him climb to safety. He took a moment to catch his breath. Nearby lay his Glock. He had a bullet in the chamber and an empty magazine. His spare was with the other gear they had set aside to lighten their load before crossing the chamber. With all the Knights gone, he wouldn't need it. He holstered his revolver and they finally made their way across the cave and into the passageway guarded by the bear-shaped stone.

They found themselves in a small cave. The tiniest glint of sunlight shone down from the ceiling high above. A long, low mound of loose stones was piled in the center of the room. Atop it lay a smooth slab of limestone. On it, someone had carved:

MARIA GONZALES
February 14, 1817 – February 23, 1836

"This must be Crockett's girlfriend," Bones said. "She died only a couple of days before the siege of the Alamo."

"How did they get here?" Kendra asked.

"I imagine not all of the tunnels were flooded back then. Hell, he might have known a back way in." He glanced up at the ceiling where a thin beam of light shone down. "But where did he stash the treasure?"

"Over there!" Kendra said.

In the shadows of an alcove on the far side of the chamber stood an iron door. They hurried over to it. There was no keyhole, only a handle. Bones grabbed hold of it and pulled. It swung open with a squeal of rusty hinges.

Behind the door was a small vault. The limestone was riddled with cracks. Water dripped from the ceiling and seeped down the walls. It looked like the whole thing might collapse at any second.

"It's empty," Kendra said.

"Almost," Bones said. A small, brass-bound chest sat in an alcove. The moment he picked it up, Bones could tell it was empty. He sat it on the floor and opened it to reveal a single sheet of paper. He picked it up carefully and held it up to the light.

Kendra read the words aloud. "You will find no mountain of gold here. David Crockett."

"I can't believe it," Bones said bitterly. "We broke the code, followed the clues, found the treasure vault, and nothing. Not a single glimmer of shiny metal."

"Here you go." Kendra was still carrying the spare oxygen tank she had used to knock out Shane. She unclipped the small canister from her belt and sat it in the alcove where the chest had been. "Metallic, shiny.

Feel better?"

"Not really, but I appreciate the effort." He carefully folded the paper and turned to leave the vault. Behind him, Kendra made a small humph.

"Bones, did you..." She began. Her words died as two figures loomed in the doorway.

Bones recognized them immediately. "No freaking way."

27

Bones could not believe his eyes. Rice and Kenneth were battered, bruised, and dripping wet, but very much alive. Each was armed with two pistols and appeared eager to use them. Kenneth's eyes were alive with a wonder bordering on ecstasy. Rice's visage was a mask of hatred.

"How the hell are you two still alive?" Bones said.

"Fell into deep water," Kenneth said. "The other two weren't so lucky."

"Both of you step out of the vault and keep your hands where I can see them," Rice ordered.

Bones and Kendra complied, slowly and moving off to the side. While Rice guarded them, Kenneth hurried over to inspect the vault.

"There's nothing there," Bones said. "Crockett left nothing but a note."

Kenneth snatched the paper from him and showed it to Rice. Their reactions could not have been more different.

"This is definitely Crockett's writing!" Kenneth said. "He really did leave the Alamo before the battle."

While Rice kept an eye on their captors, Kenneth searched the empty treasure chest, turned it over, picked it up, and gave it a shake. Next, he scrutinized every square inch of the vault.

"Nothing," he said to Rice. "No codes, no clues, and certainly no gold." His eyes fell on the grave in the middle of the chamber. He read the name aloud. "Maria Gonzales! This must be the woman Crockett fled with." He paused, scratched his head, and looked at Rice.

"Gonzales? I know it's a common surname, but any connection to the map maker?"

"An ancestor. Her sister was married to an Alamo defender." Rice's voice was cold, emotionless.

"So, if the treasure is not in the vault, where is it?" Kenneth's eyes grew wide. "Do you think he buried it with her?" He dropped to his knees and began furiously moving the pile of rocks.

Rice seemed to have little on his mind except for Crockett's message. He stared at it, lips moving as he read it over and over. Still, he appeared ready to open fire at any moment.

"Nothing here but a skeleton, tatters of clothing," Kenneth finally said. "He just laid her here and piled rocks on top of her." He stood and heaved a tired sigh. "Crockett must have kept the treasure for himself. No big surprise there."

Bones was outnumbered and outgunned. He had a pistol with a single bullet, Barney Fife with a steadier hand. He needed to improve his position. These two were authors and history nerds. He knew the type and they were easily sidetracked.

"Why are you not surprised?" Bones asked.

"One of my ancestors was among the survivors released by Santa Ana after the battle. She remembered Crockett from before the battle, all the stories he told." A shadow seemed to pass over him. His tone was harsh, his gaze flinty. "And she remembered that he did not take part in the fighting."

"That's a lie!" Rice shouted. He let Crockett's letter fall to the ground and took a few steps back, covering the exit. He now had one pistol trained on Bones and the other on Kenneth.

"Don't even try it, Rice." Kenneth had his own weapons at the ready and, like Rice, had both parties in the line of fire. Both men appeared to be at ease with their weapons, confident in their own abilities. Bad news for Bones and Kendra.

"How about one of you lend me a weapon and we can act out *The Good, The Bad, and The Ugly*?" Bones said. "I'll be Clint Eastwood and you two can fight over who's bad and who's ugly."

"Shut up," Rice said.

"Dude, we followed the map. We found the vault and there's no treasure," Bones said. "Why don't we all just get the hell out of here and get on with our lives? Personally, I'm looking forward to forgetting I ever met you two assclowns."

"Do you think this is about treasure?" Rice's voice dripped with scorn. "This is about protecting the legacy of one of history's great heroes."

"Hero?" Kenneth barked a laugh. "Dig deep enough and every hero has a skeleton in his closet."

"Or her closet," Kendra said automatically.

"You can be an imperfect person and still do great things," Bones said. He had gotten them sidetracked. Now he needed them to lose focus. "Think about it. Most of us, even people with important jobs, live ordinary lives and are quickly forgotten, but not Crockett. Odds are, he must have done something right if we still celebrate what he did."

"Big deal. People remember Hitler," Kenneth said.

"Why does everybody jump straight to Hitler these days?" Bones said.

"It's an analogy everybody understands," Kenneth said.

"Do they?" Bones asked. These days, most people had some knowledge about the Holocaust, but few knew the full story of Hitler's gradual rise to power, his message of nationalism, economic anxiety, racial division, and blaming "outsiders" for Germany's struggles in the wake of the first World War. He had even taken part in a coup in which several policemen were killed. He was convicted of treason, and his popularity outside of his most ardent supporters nosedived, but when the Great Depression hit in 1929, conditions were prime for him to make a comeback. Many years later, when the full scope of his atrocities came to light, most citizens, even those who had supported him, were astonished that they had not recognized the monster lurking inside of the man.

"What's the big deal? It's just a comparison," Kendra said.

"Once you go full Hitler you can't scale back. Things in life have degrees and nuance and context. If you compare everything to Hitler, the analogy loses its impact. Next thing you know it's, 'President Hitler won't cancel my credit card debt,' and 'Governor Hitler won't let my kid breathe in her sick classmate's sneezes.' Asshats all around."

"Crockett was not Hitler!" Rice shouted. "He was a courageous man who stood up for what was right even though it cost him his political career, and later his life."

"He obviously stole the treasure and left people to die!" Kenneth shouted. "Why are you so bent on protecting him?"

"Because Rice is one of Crockett's descendants," Bones said.

"That's not the only reason," Rice said. "People need

heroes. Stories about people who stood up for what they believed in even if it meant breaking ranks with their 'side.' Those who fought against impossible odds, even when all hope seemed lost. Heroes inspire us to greatness. It's a reality of the human condition. Why tear them down for no good reason?"

"Because truth matters! Facts matter! If we stop seeking objective truth then all we have is the competing narratives of people who want to use us," Kenneth said.

Rice laughed. "Facts? You had your mind made up about Crockett long before we found this place. You've been determined to tear him down regardless of the facts just to sell some books."

"I knew the truth, and I was right!" Kenneth shouted. "A man the Mexicans called 'Crockett' did fall in defense of the Alamo, but my ancestor saw the body and she was sure it wasn't him. He wasn't even wearing his coonskin cap."

"Stop saying that!" Rice's hands trembled.

Things were coming to a head and Bones couldn't see a way out for Kendra or himself. With his single bullet, he could eliminate one of these targets but not both. He looked around and something caught his eye. As Kenneth and Rice continued to argue, their attention now primarily focused on one another, he nudged Kendra.

"Hold onto the door and don't let go," he whispered. She blanched, swallowed hard, then did as he said. "Time to roll the dice." He drew his Glock, spun, and fired into the vault, where Kendra's oxygen canister stood in the alcove.

A massive explosion rocked the chamber. Kenneth and Rice were blown off their feet. Bones and Kendra were partially shielded from the blast, but they were both knocked down. The fragile vault collapsed. Bones and Kendra grabbed the handle of the iron door and held on as a torrent gushed forth from the vault and swept across the room, washing away the remains of Maria Gonzales. Rice and Kenneth, still stunned from the explosion, were picked up and borne out of the chamber. Their surprised shouts turned to terrified screams which seemed to last forever.

The rush of water soon slowed to a steady flow. Bones rubbed his ringing ears, checked himself for injuries. Just a few cuts and bruises. Par for the course. He helped Kendra to her feet.

"That was a hell of a lot of water," she said. "It just carried them away."

"I haven't seen someone leave a room that fast since my nephew got offered a manual labor job."

"Okay, Boomer." Kendra rolled her eyes.

Bones winced. "That was a low blow."

They walked on unsteady feet to the next chamber. Most of the floor was gone, as were many of the stalagmites, but their path to the other side remained. There was no sign of Kenneth and Rice.

"Maybe they fell into shallow water this time," Bones said.

"Let's hope. Maybe we can finally finish off this treasure hunt without anyone breathing down our necks," Kendra said.

"I hate to tell you, but I'm pretty sure the hunt is finished. The entire thing was a giant red herring. Crockett screwed over the Knights and kept the treasure for himself."

"Really?" Kendra flashed a knowing smile, reached

into her pocket. "Then why did he leave this in the bottom of the chest?" She held up a large iron key. "You were so focused on the note that you didn't even see it. I was about to tell you when Rice and Kenneth showed up."

Bones couldn't believe it. In a daze, he took the key from her, turned it over in his hand. There was no keyhole in the vault door, so what did it mean? And then it all fell into place. It was the only thing that made sense. Excited, he grabbed Kendra and planted a quick kiss on her lips. Her eyes widened in surprise, then she pulled his head down and paid him back double.

"I'm glad you're pleased," she said when they finally came up for breath. "But the fact is, we've got a key, but we don't know where the keyhole is."

Bones grinned. "I know exactly where it is."

28

For the second time in two days, Bones stood at the bottom of the old well beneath the Alamo. It was musty down here, and there was a chill in the air, but he barely noticed. Adrenaline coursed through him, and he could barely contain his excitement.

"I never thought I'd come back here," Kendra said.

"You can go back to the hotel," he said. "I told you I can handle this."

"Smartass." She elbowed him in the ribs. "You've kept me in suspense long enough. Now that we're here, will you kindly explain?"

"Crockett's letter wasn't a taunt. It was a clue." He took out his flashlight and shone it on one of the Egyptian symbols they had discovered on their previous visit. "This one, the Djew, sprang the booby trap."

"I remember it all too well," Kendra said.

"And this one turned it off." He turned his light on the symbol for the Primordial Hill.

"Keep rubbing it in," Kendra said. "There's a second bed in our hotel room and I'm not afraid to use it."

"What if I told you there was an Egyptian symbol called the Nebu, which symbolized gold?"

"I would say stop stretching this out."

"That's what she said," Bones quipped, then hurried on. "The Nebu is most closely associated with the sun god Ra, who was known as the Mountain of Gold."

"What does it look like?" she asked.

"Like a necklace draped over someone's shoulders." He traced the image in the air with his fingers.

No longer worried about drowning, they took their time searching for the symbol. They found it, covered in a layer of grime. The image was faint, but it was there.

Kendra gave it a shove. The stone gave way, and a loud rumbling filled the well. They immediately looked around to see if she had sprung another trap.

"Didn't you learn anything last time?" Bones said.

"Somebody had to push it. Might as well be me."

To their relief, a section of wall swung back, revealing a short tunnel that led to an iron door. Kendra let out a gasp of delight and kissed him on the cheek.

"We found it!" Her smile evaporated "Unless there's another clue behind that door."

"You've watched *National Treasure* too many times," Bones said, taking out the key and handing it to her.

"You can't watch that movie too many times," she said. "It keeps getting better." She fitted the key into the keyhole and froze. She glanced back at Bones. "Ready?" She gave the key a twist.

It didn't budge.

"Try the other direction," Bones suggested.

"Like I wasn't going to?" She turned the key in the other direction. It rotated a shrill half a turn. She took a deep breath and pushed the door open.

"Holy crap," Bones said.

The small vault held six wooden chests. Kendra opened the closest one. It was filled with coins! Another held gold and silver nuggets.

"There must be a fortune down here!" Kendra exclaimed. "Have you ever seen anything like it?"

But Bones' attention had been drawn to something else. A coonskin cap hung on the wall just above the treasure chests.

"You have got to be freaking kidding me. That crafty, brave son of a bitch."

"What is it?" Kendra asked. "Is that Crockett's hat?"

"I think so."

"Why would he leave it in here?" she asked.

"To make sure whoever found the treasure knew that he came back for the battle." The seemingly conflicting accounts of Crockett's final days might not have conflicted at all. "I think Crockett was charged with keeping the treasure away from Santa Ana. It would have been a difficult and risky proposition to move this much treasure on short notice and with enemies all around. He could have easily lost the treasure to the Spanish, local natives, or roving bandits. Instead, he left it in its vault, where it was protected by the booby trap you so cleverly discovered, and created the treasure hunt as a cover."

"Why leave a key in Jacob's Hole?" Kendra asked.

"He must have known there was a good chance there would be no survivors of the battle. He had to leave a trail that initiates could follow.."

"Even if it meant going in a circle," Kendra said.

"Which is exactly what he did. After seizing the opportunity to save the woman he loved from the coming battle, she died just as the siege was beginning. He had completed his mission, so there was no reason for him not to come back and join the fight. He sneaked past enemy lines, infiltrated the Alamo, and hung his trademark cap here to prove he had done it."

"It sounds plausible," Kendra admitted.

"Think about it," Bones said. "Everybody knows Crockett died at the Alamo. The only question is whether he was killed in combat or if he lived long enough to be captured and executed."

"Rice and Kenneth were both right!" Kendra said. "Just think, if they had helped us instead of trying to kill us, both could have written bestsellers, Rice could preserve Crockett's good name, and we could have split the treasure. There's plenty to go around." She hesitated. "Do we get to keep any of it?"

"They'll say it's public property, which means it belongs to the state. Besides, we don't want to be associated with the death of the security guard."

"And it won't be long before this place is found," Kendra said. "Probably the next time someone opens the secret room inside the mission."

"In that case, we need to make sure it's found by the right person. I'm thinking a televisions producer. If we can't get a cut of the treasure, we can share in the proceeds from the documentary."

"You know anyone like that?"

"Let me see." Bones made a show of scrolling through the contacts on his phone. "Joanna Slater, maybe."

"I thought she was eaten by a crocodile," Kendra said.

"No, she lived. But I think we need an American for this one. Somebody with a lot of connections." He scrolled to the name Grizzly Grant. "Perfect! I'll text him when we get back above ground."

"Are you going to tell him there's a vault down here with five treasure chests or shall we let it be a surprise?"

"You mean six treasure chests."

"Not if you help me carry one of them out of here." She waggled her eyebrows. "We're the ones who put our lives at risk to find it. And what the government doesn't know won't hurt them."

Bones couldn't help but laugh.

"Kendra, you are a woman after my own heart!"

The End

If you enjoyed *Alamo Gold*, try *Treasure of the Dead*! Bones and Maddock head to Haiti in search of a lost treasure and come face-to-face with something they've never seen before!

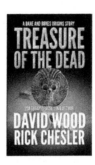

SEVEN FREE EBOOKS!

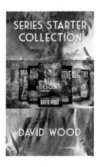

Get the entire *David Wood Series Starter Collection* for free when you subscribe to his newsletter! Visit his website to get book one of the *Dane Maddock, Bones Bonebrake, Brock Stone, Jade Ihara, Jake Crowley, Sam Aston,* and *Myrmidons* series all in one ebook bundle!
www.davidwoodweb.com

About the Author

David Wood is the USA Today bestselling author of the action-adventure series, The Dane Maddock Adventures, and many other works. He also writes fantasy under his David Debord pen name and science fiction as Finn Gray. He's a member of International Thriller Writers and the Horror Writers Association. David and his family live in Santa Fe, New Mexico. Visit him online at www.davidwoodweb.com and get a free reader's guide to the Dane Maddock universe and his other works.